THE ROLLING HEADS

Also by Aaron Marc Stein

THE ROLLING HEADS
CHILL FACTOR
NOWHERE?
LEND ME YOUR EARS
COFFIN COUNTRY
BODY SEARCH
LOCK AND KEY
THE FINGER
ALP MURDER
KILL IS A FOUR-LETTER WORD
SNARE ANDALUCIAN
DEADLY DELIGHT
I FEAR THE GREEKS
BLOOD ON THE STARS
HOME AND MURDER
NEVER NEED AN ENEMY
SITTING UP DEAD
MOONMILK AND MURDER
DEATH MEETS 400 RABBITS
THE DEAD THING IN THE POOL
MASK FOR MURDER
PISTOLS FOR TWO
SHOOT ME DACENT
FRIGHTENED AMAZON
THREE-WITH BLOOD
DAYS OF MISFORTUNE
THE SECOND BURIAL
THE CRADLE AND THE GRAVE
WE SAW HIM DIE
. . . AND HIGH WATER
THE CASE OF THE ABSENT-MINDED PROFESSOR
ONLY THE GUILTY
UP TO NO GOOD
THE SUN IS A WITNESS
HER BODY SPEAKS
SPIRALS

THE ROLLING HEADS

AARON MARC STEIN

PUBLISHED FOR THE CRIME CLUB BY
DOUBLEDAY & COMPANY, INC.
GARDEN CITY, NEW YORK
1979

All of the characters in this book
are fictitious, and any resemblance
to actual persons, living or dead,
is purely coincidental.

ISBN: 0-385-14643-4
Library of Congress Catalog Card Number 78–69671

Printed in the United States of America
First Edition

For
Beaujolais
without her I'd never
have known Mathilda
and
for
her amanuensis
Peter Poor

THE
ROLLING HEADS

I.

Thank God for girls. He did, after all, make them, even if the Devil takes them. I'm not ungrateful, but there are times when I could wish that along with the lovelies He'd furnished us guys with some kind of built-in defenses. You know me—one Matthew Erridge, known as Matt. I'm a big boy. Let's say I'm a decent interval past being a kid. There are those who would say I'm old enough to know better, but heaven forbid that I should ever be that old. I've been through it too many times, and this much I've learned about myself: I'll never know better, not this side of the grave, even though time and again, through entanglement with a luscious female, I've come uncomfortably close to it.

Let me explain. I'm an engineer. Occasionally I hit a job in some properly populated area, one adequately peopled with folk of the female persuasion. More often than not, however, I do my work in places where even men are few, and women fewer or not at all. If a man goes steady with the opportunity for folly, he may be expected to exercise some measure of sanity and restraint. When a guy who's been starving is turned loose in the midst of plenty, are you going to criticize him for overeating?

When I say the midst of plenty, I mean Dinard. I'm not going to tell you much about Dinard. It's never been my kind of place. If it weren't for the fact that it was in Dinard that the madness first set in, I wouldn't be mentioning it at all. I'd gone there to talk to a man about a job. In engineering the guys who control the best jobs are likely to be the fattest of fat cats. In my experience those cats come in two varieties.

There are those who can't bear to be too far from their money. That kind lives behind a desk in Zurich or New York or Houston or Tokyo. If you do business with them, it's quickly done. For them time is money, and they like to lavish as little as possible of either on the hired hands.

On this occasion my fat cat was of the other type. For his kind time is a nuisance. He runs all over the world, trying to use it up and, wherever he goes, always lands in the same place. The place may be called Marbella or Palm Springs or Sardinia or Palm Beach or Las Vegas or Deauville or Nassau or Monte Carlo. For this guy it was called Dinard. Do you know Dinard? It's on the north coast of Brittany, the part of it the French call the Côte d'Émeraude. If you range along that stretch of coast, giving Dinard a wide berth, you can think they call it that because it's so green and so beautiful. If you hang out in Dinard during the season, you can think it's because emeralds are what the girls wear when they are wearing anything more than a bikini. I've seen some take cover under both the bikini and the emeralds, and for them the emeralds cover more skin.

You are not going to find many places in France that are less French than Dinard. In a country where even the smallest of villages is likely to drip with history, Dinard has none. It's brand-new. It was started by an American about 1850. American and British money quickly wiped away all traces of the little fishing village that had been there. What they've put in its place is great if you're filthy rich and you want to be in France without ever for a moment feeling that you've left home.

There are the beaches. There are the grand hotels. There are the big, plush villas. There's the Casino. More than anything, there is the Casino. It looks like what might have been spawned out of the mating of an opera house and a stock exchange, and for my fat cat the Casino was the whole of Dinard. Dinard? It was the whole of France. It was the world.

I'm not going to bore you with an account of his winnings and losings. I'm not even going to bore you with him. I was never able to catch him out of the Casino long enough to get him down to talking about the job. So once I'd put it across to him that I was available, I was ready to haul away from Dinard. If he ever came around to taking his mind off baccarat, he could send his minions out to find me.

Once I'd come to that decision, I should have headed straight for the Porsche and been on the move. That's great country and it's a great stretch of coast. Rolling along in Baby, I wouldn't have had to go far to find myself a spot that was more my kind of place.

So why did I choose to stay another night and not pull out till morning? Need I tell you? There was a girl. I had been there only a few days, but I had become something of an authority on the Dinard girls. Waiting around on the Grande Plage till my man came out of the Casino to take a breather from baccarat, I'd had some good long stretches of girl-watching, and it had quickly narrowed down to watching one girl.

It began with a mistake. Of course, it was a mistake all the way through, but we're coming to that. First things first.

I had come to Dinard late at night. The first I'd been out and about was the early morning of the next day when I was taking a before-breakfast swim. Coming out of the water onto the beach, I thought at that hour I had the Grande Plage all to myself.

I was shaking the water out of my ears when I first heard her calling me. It wasn't only that she was calling me, she was using a tone nobody had used on Erridge since way back in the days when he was a boy soprano. It was a woman's voice and, even though it was noticeably harsh with annoyance and anger, it was still sweet music.

"Matt," she was shouting. "Come here, Matt. I said come here. Don't go pretending you don't hear me. Come here at once. Didn't you hear what I said? Come away from that nasty thing. I'm not going to tell you again."

Nasty thing? I had nothing to come away from but my beach towel.

"Matt," she started up again. "I'm warning you, Matt. You're getting me angry. You just wait till I get my hands on you. You'll be sorry."

Looking around, I located the source of the threat. It was a girl. There was nobody else in sight. She was down the beach and she was looking straight at me. Her gestures matched her words. She was at once beckoning and threatening. She was nobody I knew, but she was someone I could stand knowing. She wasn't wearing a bikini and she wasn't festooned with emeralds. She was wearing tight pants, and if they don't make a woman look absurd, they make her look like something that would summon lust out of a stone. Erridge, in case you don't know, is not a stone. He lusts on far slighter provocation. With the pants, she was wearing one of those little shirts they were going in for that summer. They look as though they swiped them from a very small brother. There's not enough shirt to allow it to come together in front. They fasten it with one button below the navel, and what's framed in the V is never less than eye-catching. What was framed in her V took my breath away.

So there she was standing with the wind playing tricks in her hair, such tricks as I could have enjoyed playing myself, and she was telling me to wait till she got her hands on me. I saw no reason to wait. It had been far too long since anything that breathtaking had her hands on me. A man gets a promise like that. Does he dawdle? Does he delay? He does not. He moves straight to it.

I moved, and she appeared to be taking no notice of my docility. She just went on shouting her summonses and her threats. Remembering way back, I was finding it a familiar sound. I was recalling those occasions when mounting irritation brought about a shift from calling me Matt to using the more formal Matthew. "Matthew" used to mean I was in real trouble.

She made the shift, but it wasn't to Matthew.

"Mathilda," she shouted. "You stop pretending you don't know I'm talking to you. I've had enough of your nonsense, Mathilda."

Maybe that should have stopped me, but I made a quick decision. I didn't have to let on that I'd caught those Mathildas. I did have the impulse to look back over my shoulder to try to catch a glimpse of the erring Mathilda, but I resisted it. Even one backward glance could have been a giveaway, and opportunity doesn't knock all that often.

I kept going till I was within speaking distance. I worked at ignoring the fact that she was taking no notice of my advance. I said nothing till I'd come up right beside her.

"You were talking to me, ma'am," I said.

She took time out before answering. It was time for a cool appraisal, one of those eye-travels-from-head-to-foot jobs that takes in everything in between.

"You," she said, having taken all of me in. "Why would I speak to you?"

"Just the question I've been asking myself. I thought maybe you'd tell me."

"I wasn't talking to you."

"You called me."

She worked at suppressing a smile. Her lips twitched, and for a moment a dimple made a flickering appearance.

"You're called Mathilda?" she asked.

"Matthew," I said. "People who know me call me Matt."

"I don't know you, so it's no good your coming to heel. It's *her* I want."

Her look slipped past my shoulder and keyed to something down the beach. I turned and looked. There was a dog down there. It looked like about a meter's length of chunky, low-slung basset. It was nuzzling something in the sand. From where I had been while I was toweling off, I hadn't seen it. From that angle it had been hidden behind one of those small towers that during normal swimming hours serve as observation perches for lifeguards. I had gone in at an hour before the lifeguards came on duty.

"I'll go down and get her for you," I offered.

"What are you? The local dogcatcher?"

"More like a visiting Boy Scout," I said. "I like to get my day's good deed out of the way early. It leaves me the rest of the day for having fun."

She unbent.

"You can help me catch her if you like," she said.

"I like."

We walked over the sand together. She said nothing. If there was to be conversation, it was falling to me to make it.

"You call me Matt," I said. "What do I call you?"

"Do you have to call me?"

"I do lots of things I don't have to do. They're the best things."

"You must do this a lot," she said. "You're so glib about it."

"I've been practicing," I told her, "working it up against the day when there might be someone like you."

"Smooth," she murmured. "You don't look smooth."

"I am a complex personality, worth exploring."

She laughed.

"People call me Barbie," she said.

"Do I have to worry about Ken?" I asked.

"Yes," she said. "You have to worry. You wouldn't be playing with dolls."

"That's okay," I said. "I've never played with dolls. I'd rather worry."

We were closing in on Mathilda. She dropped the thing she'd been nuzzling. It was a washed-up starfish. Looking back at us with a broad grin, Mathilda took off. She went full tilt, and the speed of her running had her long, silky ears streaming flat past her shoulders. We went after her, but with every step she was widening the gap. Then, looking back at us, she would stop and grin while she waited for us to catch up. When she was only just out of reach, she took off again. I made a dive for her, but she slid off my fingertips as I smacked belly-down in the sand.

That was a game she could have kept going all day. It was all right with me except for the fact that, chasing her, we had nothing left over for talk or anything else. Being with Barbie was great, but of all the things a man might like to do when he's having time with a girl, dog chasing falls somewhere near the bottom of the list.

I circled in a wide arc to head the pup off. Barbie stayed on course. Between us we were closing in on Mathilda. It was the old reliable pincer movement, but Mathilda knew her strategy. She wasn't waiting for us to close the net. Again she held it, grinning at us, until we were just within fingertip reach. One more step and we could grab. She didn't wait for that one more step, no canine Cannae for her. With a lightning, ninety-degree turn—that dog could turn on a dime, if you can imagine an elongated dime—she dashed into the water.

With her close-to-the-ground build, she was almost immediately into her swimming depth. I splashed in after her, and that was where she'd miscalculated. What was swimming depth for her was little more than ankle-deep for me. She had taken herself into an element where I had the speed advantage over her. I reached down and scooped her up.

I had myself braced for handling a double armful of squirming animal, but Mathilda was a dog without illusions. The game was over and she knew it. For a dog of her cheerful disposition, however, the end of one game was only the beginning of another. Settling herself comfortably with her forepaws on my chest, she put everything she had into licking my face. Maybe it was love at first sight, and maybe she liked the taste of the sea salt I had drying on my skin.

Barbie was waiting for us at the water's edge. She snapped the leash onto Mathilda's collar. A quick "thanks" was all she had for me before she launched into talking seriously to Mathilda. We walked back across the beach together, but all the way she was fully occupied with telling Mathilda that she was a bad dog. Mathilda was ungrateful. She was unmindful of all the money Barbie had spent on all those lessons at obedience school. It was no good Mathilda's pretending that she didn't know what it meant when Barbie told her to heel. Mathilda knew exactly what it meant and Barbie knew she knew it. There was no construction that could be put on her behavior but that it was deliberate disobedience. Wasn't Mathilda ashamed of herself?

As we walked up the beach with Mathilda on a slack leash, she waddled after us docilely. Her front end was suitably contrite. Her big brown eyes implored forgiveness. She hung her head. Her long, velvet ears trailed in the sand. Her dewlaps sagged despondently. Her aft end all the while was leading a life of its own. There was something jaunty about the waddle back there, and her tail wagged merrily.

"I'm a bad dog," said one end.

"But isn't it fun?" said the other.

"It may be no good talking to her," I said. "Only half of her is listening."

"No part of her is listening," Barbie said. "I know her. She's just putting on an act."

"Have you and Mathilda had breakfast?" I asked.

"We don't eat breakfast."

"No breakfast? In this country no breakfast? Croissant, brioche, Normandy butter, Breton honey, Reine Claude jam, coffee, chocolate. Isn't it time that Mathilda learned that there are things more palatable than starfish? Isn't it time that you learned you are in France and that breakfast in France is for the gods even here in Dinard, which is hardly France at all?"

"The gods can have it," Barbie said. "It goes on the hips."

"Gods don't have hips."

"So they can eat breakfast."

"You *do* eat lunch," I persisted.

"We eat lunch with Ken."

"And dinner?"

"With Ken."

"Apéritifs?"

"With Ken."

"Midmorning coffee," I babbled. "Afternoon tea, cocktails, midnight snacks, nightcaps?"

"Do you eat straight through the day?" she asked.

"I drink a lot of the time," I said.

"Watch it," she said. "You don't want to get fat. You're nice the way you are."

"Since I'm nice, when do I see you again?"

"You'll see me around," she said, "with Ken."

"It's obvious that Mathilda isn't a one-man dog. You're not a one-man woman, are you?"

"I'm not an any-guy-that-comes-along woman."

"That goes even for dogcatchers?"

"Mathilda has already rewarded you, and I said thank you."

With that she strode off. Mathilda followed after, but now not on a slack leash. Now Mathilda needed pulling. The pup kept looking back at me. Her look was questioning. I could read the question.

"Are you a guy who gives up that easily?" she was asking me.

I did see the girl around. The first time was that same afternoon in the Casino. She didn't have Mathilda with her there. She was at the baccarat table, sitting right alongside my fat cat, but don't get any ideas. She hadn't taken up with him either. There was another man at her other side. From the way he was bird-dogging her chips, I had to figure that he would be Ken.

He didn't fit the Ken stereotype. Kens don't have jowls that stay blue even when clean-shaven. Kens don't have hair that's begun to thin on top. Kens have sideburns, but theirs aren't flecked with gray. Kens don't have a scar that throws one eyebrow slightly out of line. Kens are well-muscled, but they aren't burly. They look as though they could handle themselves, but they don't look as though they were itching to handle every guy that comes along. Kens don't look mean.

"Hello," I said.

She looked over her shoulder and promptly looked back at the baccarat table even as she was answering my hello.

"How's Mathilda?" I asked.

"Mathilda's fine," she said without turning away from the table.

"She been asking for me?"

"No."

"I can't believe that. Mathilda and I, we have a thing going."

"Anything that has fur on it Mathilda falls for. Don't let it go to your head."

Ken got to his feet. He was scowling.

"Move it, buddy," he said. "Can't you see you're annoying the lady?"

He was wearing one of those striped shirts the fishermen used to wear before some high tide swept the shirts into the boutiques. She grabbed a fistful of the bottom of it and tugged. She wanted him to sit back down.

"Relax, Johnny. The gentleman isn't annoying me."

He didn't respond to the tug. He balled up his fists.

"So he's annoying *me,*" he said.

My fat cat spoke up.

"That's a pity," he purred, "since the gentleman is my guest and nobody moves my guests on. Maybe you'd like to take your play to one of the other tables."

The words were plain enough, but they were nothing to the fat cat's tone. It was the guy up in the castle talking to the dirt down in the muck. It was telling the man he was dirt. It was telling him to mind his manners. It was telling him to remember his place.

I thought, at the least, it was going to win my man a thick lip. I had myself poised to move in on Johnny. After all, if there was to be a fight, it was *my* fight. I couldn't let Mr. Fat Cat take it on for me. The fisherman's shirt was too tight for the lug to be carrying anything under it but that conspicuous lot of bulging muscles. The jeans he had on with it were tight as well, but not so tight that there couldn't have been a knife stuck in his boot-top. There was everything about the man to say that he might carry a gun, and more to say he was the type that might prefer a knife.

Nothing happened. Big and ugly just sat down.

"Yes, Mr. Elston," he said. "I didn't know he was your guest, Mr. Elston. That's all right then, Mr. Elston."

He was groveling. So now I knew something more about this Johnny. He was also the type to crawl on his belly to the big bucks, a born lackey born too late for the age when the rich and the powerful carried retinues of lackeys around with them.

I hung on awhile watching the play, but that wasn't much fun. I hauled out of the Casino to watch the girls on the beach instead. In the afternoon the beach is full of girls, but they weren't much fun either. None of them was Barbie and, since I was having her on my mind, nothing out there looked good enough.

When I saw her again that evening, it wasn't quite by accident. It was after dinner and a good, warm summer night. There was a moon on the water and the sky was crowded with stars that were even bright enough to hold their own against the glare of the café lights on Dinard's shorefront.

She was at a café table with the lug she called Johnny. I would have gone by and never seen them if it hadn't been for Mathilda. Mathilda came running out from between the tables with her tail wagging. If you want to see a tail wag a dog, you'd have to know Mathilda. When hers really gets to wagging, there is so much oomph in it that at least half of her considerable length wags with it.

Heading straight for me, she jumped up at me in an effort to lick my face. I suppose she had no way of knowing that I'd showered and shaved since I'd last been in swimming and she wasn't going to find me deliciously salty. She couldn't quite make it that high. She settled for waddling alongside me and, between waddles, climbing my trouser leg to lick my hand.

Guessing that where she was there would also be Barbie, I looked back. Barbie was there and she was wearing an evening version of what she had worn earlier in the day. I mean this time the shirt swiped from very small brother gave just as much in the V, and it also gave a lot more. This one was of filmy silk. It was see-through stuff. What there was to see should have been against the law. To let a guy see it when he isn't permitted to touch must rate as cruel and unusual punishment.

I turned around and walked back to the café. Mathilda, after all, was going where I went, and I wasn't about to set myself up in the pupnaping business. There was an empty table a couple removed from the one where Barbie was settled in with her Johnny. I took it. It suited Mathilda fine. She could gambol happily back and forth between their table and mine. I ordered coffee and a calvados, and I sat there taking in the view. If you're asking, Which view? you're just not human. That's one thing Erridge is. It's even been said he's too human.

They were having an argument. I couldn't hear what they were saying. They were holding it at a low pitch, but it showed in their faces and in the way they were spitting the words at each other. I worked on my coffee and calvados and I had myself a bit of daydream. She was going to get fed up with him. She was going to get up from his table and come over to join me at mine. It was going to be the beginning of a great evening. After all, the lug was asking for it, and Mathilda was working on it. Didn't I have everything going for me?

The argument kept heating up. It climaxed with Barbie hauling off and landing an openhanded slap on the guy's cheek. She hit him a good one. I could tell from the sound of it and from the way the print of fingers and palm first showed white against his bluish jowl and then turned an angry red. He jumped to his feet and raised his hand. He had started the swing that was going to fetch her a backhander that would knock her off her seat, but I reached him first and hooked my arm through his. From the way the crook of his elbow came up hard against mine, I had a good estimate of the force he'd been putting into the lick he'd have aimed at her. If it had landed, it could just about have knocked her head off.

Mathilda pushed herself in between our feet and just sat there, wagging her tail and grinning up at us. For that crazy dog there wasn't anything that wouldn't be a game. She was going to be a problem. The two of us were about to tangle. Having that much yardage of dog right there in the middle of things was going to complicate the footwork.

We stood that way for just a moment or two, and then the only thing that couldn't have been expected happened. All his rage just drained out of Johnny. A sickly smile replaced it. Turning, he slid his arm free and laid it across my shoulders. Holding it there, he gave me a friendly squeeze.

"Thanks, buddy," he said. "I'd have hated myself for that."

If the turnabout knocked me over, it seemed to be having no less effect on Barbie. Her mouth dropped open. She blinked up at us a couple of times. Recovering from her astonishment, she hauled up her lower jaw and ran the tip of her tongue over her lips. She started to speak, but she had trouble finding her voice. She swallowed hard in search of it.

"Go away, Matt," she said.

Johnny shook his head. He still had his arm around my shoulders. He was holding me tight against him.

"No," he said. "I'm buying the man a drink."

"Go away, Matt," she repeated.

I shrugged myself out from under Johnny's arm.

"The lady calls the shots," I said.

Johnny let it go.

"Thanks anyway," he said.

"Anytime," I mumbled and moved off.

Mathilda moved with me. I stopped and talked to her. She was in no mood to listen. Maybe she wanted me to go back and let her buy me a drink. I walked her back to their table. They had their heads together now, and it was more than just holding it low. They were whispering. I broke in on it.

"I can't talk Mathilda out of following me," I said. "You'll have to put her on the leash."

Johnny grabbed her by the collar. I didn't like the way he hauled on it, but Barbie snapped the leash to the collar and he took his hand away. She said nothing to me. She was just talking to Mathilda.

"You keep on cutting up this way," she said, "and you're going to have to go back to obedience school."

I took off. I wasn't at all certain that he wouldn't be beating the whatsis out of her as soon as he got her alone, but there seemed to be nothing I could do about it. As I saw it, she was either sucking around for it and who was I to spoil her fun, or else she knew her man and she had everything under control. There had been that moment when he'd been swinging on her, of course, but there had also been his quick turnabout. It was possible that she knew that, aware of how close he'd come, he would now be afraid of it and, for a while at least, there would be nothing that could make him explode.

I went into the Casino and watched Elston play for a while. I even got myself some chips and had a go at it. I had some winnings and there wasn't any lift in that. Then I had some losings and they didn't get to me either. Pretty soon I was back to winning and it seemed impolite to stay there yawning in the croupier's face. I cashed in my chips, pocketed my profit, and pulled away.

The night was still fairly young. I walked back to the café, but they weren't there any more. I stopped and had a calvados, and then another, and then too many. Eventually I gave up on it and went to bed. In the morning I woke feeling like a slow-study Sir Isaac Newton. It took only one apple dropping on his head for him to discover gravitation. I felt as though apples had been falling on my pate all night, and I was discovering nothing.

I needed a quick swim to clear my head. It was early, even earlier than the day before. The sun was only just breaking the horizon and this was midsummer in the north of France, a time when in those parts nights are short. I expected I would have the Grande Plage all to myself, but I had no more than hit the beach when Mathilda was jumping all over me. On this day, however, things were different. Barbie wasn't calling her to heel. Barbie was there. She was sitting on the sand with yards and yards of thick robe wrapped around her. She spoke first.

"Good morning," she said. "I've been waiting for you."

"I didn't know. The last thing you said was, 'Go away.'"

"I suppose that was rude."

"It wasn't flattering and it wasn't kind."

"Will it be flattering if I say I'll feel safer swimming if I can swim with you?"

She got up off the sand and let the robe drop away. I'd been ready for something like a new record in bikini skimpiness, but there was no bikini at all. There was nothing, not even a pasty.

"If feeling safer includes feeling safe from me," I said, "I don't know that I'd call that flattering."

"We have the beach to ourselves," she said. "You're overdressed."

We went skinny dipping. Anything she said about not feeling safe going in alone was a crock. That baby could swim. She was as easy and as comfortable and as natural in the water as she was in the Casino at the baccarat table. We had a couple of hours for it. Then, when the sun was well up and the time was approaching when we'd no longer have the Grande Plage to ourselves, she hit her beach bag and brought out a bikini. We climbed into our minimal cover and lay on the sand enjoying the feel of the early-morning sun as it gathered its strength. We couldn't have been more relaxed. We even slept some. My head was back to normal and all was right with my world.

"Breakfast," Barbie said.

"Hips. I thought you never ate it."

"Today's different. Swimming makes me hungry."

Over breakfast she broached what she had in mind.

"I thought you'd be curious about last night," she said.

"You came close to getting your head knocked off."

"He was sorry."

"So he said."

"But not sorry enough."

"What's 'enough'? "

"Not enough to do what I asked."

I know a cue when one is thrown at me. I was expected to ask what he had refused her. I was expected to follow with offering to provide it, whatever it might be. Caution gave way to curiosity.

"And what was that?" I asked.

"Little enough," she said. "I'm sick of stupid Dinard. I'm sick of the stupid Casino. I'm sick of being in France and not going anywhere or seeing anything. Was it too much to ask for him to take me to Mont St. Michel?"

"At Mont St. Michel you drown in tourists."

"You've been?"

"I've been."

"And it's not what it's cracked up to be?"

"It's everything it's cracked up to be and more. The trouble is that it's been cracked up so much that it's covered all over with sightseers. It's a Norman Coney Island."

"I bet if Mathilda asked you, you'd take us."

"If *you* ask me, I'll take you."

"I'm asking."

"What about Ken?"

"Who's Ken?"

"You call him 'Johnny.'"

"Oh, him! Are you afraid of him?"

"I'm not, but I think maybe *you* ought to be."

"He won't care. He won't even know I'm gone. He has the Casino. He doesn't need me. I distract him from his gambling."

"That's not what you told me yesterday."

"That was yesterday. Do you want to live in the past?"

II.

She could have been right about her Johnny and she could have been wrong, but what she was saying about him certainly went for my fat cat. I checked in with him by phone and told him I was taking off for a couple of days. I told him I'd be in touch. If he saw a day coming up when he might have time for me, he could just say the word and we could set something up. I couldn't be sure he was even listening. This was morning. The guy was never really awake till afternoon, opening time at the Casino. Most of what I heard over the phone was yawn, but he did tell me to run along and have myself some fun.

There was still a lot of morning left when we hit the road down to Dinan. From Dinard to the Mont it's only about fifty miles, and for Baby that's like nothing. Since Barbie was bent on going places and seeing things, we made all the stops en route—Dinan for Duchess Anne's Dungeon and the Basilica that didn't let its right side know what its left was doing. In Dol-de-Bretagne it was the enormous granite cathedral. Just across the line in Normandy we went into Pontorson for the church William the Conqueror built in thanks for having been saved from the quicksands over by Mont St. Michel. Since it was Saxon Harold who saved him, and we all know how he paid Harold off, I suppose he had to thank somebody.

When I told Barbie about that, she said William must have been a bastard, which was a good guess any way you take it. Even with all those stops, we were parked on the sands at the foot of the Mont in time to walk through the gate to that hotel just inside the walls, check in, and hit the dining room for an early lunch.

Barbie had never heard of Cancale oysters. It was a great lunch. I like girls with a lot to learn. We were left with plenty of afternoon for the long climb up the ramps past the souvenir shops, the picture postcard vendors, and the crêperies. At the top I took her into the abbey and, dodging the guided tours, showed her through the whole works myself.

It's a great place even if you do have to see it past the tourist swarm. Those old Normans were the toughest of the medieval tough babies, and the way they saw their St. Michael, he was even tougher than them. They built him an abbey that spoke for strength and guts, layer on layer of columns and arches and vaults to support the incredible weight of all those superimposed layers, and to do it without any sign of heaviness or of strain. No engineer can look at it without feeling humbled.

I was able to let it run away with me because Barbie was taking it all in and never showing the first sign of being tired or bored. Mathilda followed along and behaved herself. I can't say she wasn't bored. It was obvious she had a preference for the places we'd hit on the way over from Dinard. They had more interesting smells.

We came down in time for a drink on the ramparts while the sun, setting over the surrounding tidal flats, was bringing a blush out of the famous quicksands. Barbie insisted on changing for dinner and, since she had held out for separate rooms, what she put on was unfair. I've already told you what she did for pants. I can't say she did any more for a dress, because there is no more, but the way she hit you with it in a dress was a fresh and different impact.

Dinner was long and comforting, what with lobsters and salt-marsh lamb, and a dessert omelette only slightly smaller than a blimp and so good that we ate almost the whole of it. Mathilda did her part, wolfing down the impossible excess. We lingered over coffee and calvados and then the moon was up, and only the dullest clod would have not been for a stroll along the ramparts. Even if Mathilda hadn't needed a run, the moonlight and the illuminations of the abbey would have demanded it.

We strolled. Much of the great tide of tourists had, of course, pulled out. Over our drinks at sunset we had seen the great battalions of buses load up and trundle off, but the Mont hadn't emptied. The hotel dining room had been full at dinner, and the hotel bar had been jumping. It couldn't have been much different in all the other hotels, but astonishingly, we seemed to be having the ramparts to ourselves.

We were meeting nobody. We were alone with the moon and the stars, the buttresses and the machicolations, and St. Michael spotlighted atop the crown of his towering abbey. Passing through a vaulted strongpoint, we came into an area of all but total darkness. Narrow slabs of damped-down moonlight did come through the embrasures where once the archers stood guard, but otherwise it was all black. I was leading the way, and Barbie was coming after with a hand resting on my shoulder.

There was a moment of muffled sound and the hand came away. I turned to reach for her. I reached, but I never touched. The bony edge of a forearm hit hard against my throat. I knew how to handle that. Grab at the arm as you pivot inside it. If you can make it to clamp your hand on just the right spot, you have a choice. You can send your man hurtling over your head or you can break his arm.

My man knew as much as I did. Even as I was making

my grab and starting my pivot, his thumb found one of those trigger points where firm pressure produces instantaneous blackout. I know he found it and I know he pressed because I did black out. A man goes out, but he has to be in poor shape if he is to stay out long. Erridge is in good shape, and Mathilda was there to lend a helping hand.

You want accuracy? Okay. Mathilda lent a helping tongue. She was running up and down my crumpled body, licking my face and my hands. En route between face and hands she was whimpering excitedly. There are various methods for bringing an unconscious man back to his senses. Moisture and massage add up to one of the ways of doing it. I came to and scrambled to my feet. Mathilda ran off and came back, ran off and came back. I could follow her by the sound of her constant whimpering, and I could hear the click of her toenails against the stones of the battlement floor.

I had no flashlight on me. I had to make do with the flame of my cigarette lighter. It wasn't much, but it was enough to show me that I was still in that vaulted strongpoint and I was alone. Barbie was gone and my attacker was gone. There was nothing to tell me which way. I had to go on probabilities alone, and probabilities said that it would be back the way we had come. There would be nothing up ahead but the ramps and the steps and locked doors all the way to the abbey entrance, and that would also be locked for the night. There was only one exit from the Mont. There was the single gate down in the surrounding wall. It gave on the sands and the causeway.

I headed out of the strongpoint in that direction. In the moonlight I could see Mathilda. She was running ahead and stopping to see if I was following. When I paused, she ran back to me and whimpered and then ran ahead again.

On her forward runs she kept her head down, her nose all but touching the paving stones. If she wasn't tracking, she was putting on a great imitation of it.

I followed where she was leading. Probability had said it would be the way, and now Mathilda was backing up probability. I broke into a run and she ran ahead of me. I talked to St. Michael as I ran.

"Make that pup know what she's doing," I was asking. "Don't let her be playing games."

She came to a place that demanded a choice. Straight ahead would be a short run into another strongpoint that would be a dead end. A sharp right led to a door that gave on the third floor of the hotel. When we had gone out for our stroll, the *concièrge* had told us he was about to lock up. He explained that we could come back in by this door to the third floor that opened directly off the ramparts. That one was never locked. I had been amused by a locking-up process that would be that half-assed, but now I was no longer amused.

There was a third possibility—a flight of stone steps that led down off the ramparts to the Grande Rue, the locked main entrance of the hotel, and beyond it the King's Gate and the sands and the causeway.

Mathilda ignored the straight run into the strongpoint's dead end. She hesitated briefly between the right-hand turn to the hotel's upstairs door and the stairs down to the Grande Rue. After a brief sniffing at one and then the other, she settled for the stairs. I ran down behind her, hard on her haunches. Down in the Grande Rue she showed no hesitation. She went streaking for the King's Gate.

She was through it well before me and, as I ran to catch up with her, I could hear her out there, barking her head off. Mathilda has a basso bark. She pulls it up all the way from her hind paws. It resonates through the full extension of that long body of hers. It's an operatic bark, a sound built to fill vast spaces.

I came bursting out the gate and Mathilda was there. She was back to the way she had begun. She was running forward, pausing to look back for me, and running back only to wheel and run forward again. She was giving out with those great resonant barks all the while.

Apart from Mathilda's frenzy and the soft stirrings of the water, there was only one other thing moving out there. I could see the lights of a speeding car. It was roaring away down the causeway. Calling Mathilda, I dashed for Baby. If it comes to a chase, there isn't much on wheels that Baby can't catch. That's a great length of causeway across the quicksands and the tidal flats, and after the causeway there are kilometers of road down toward Pontorson, and a good piece of it without the first turnoff.

I jumped into Baby, vaulting the door, but then I had to open it for Mathilda to make her jump. She's a great dog, but she was never made to be a high jumper. She's built too close to the ground.

I wanted to give Baby the gun, but I had to hold her down until we were off the sand and onto the solid pavement of the causeway. As it was, we sent tall fans of sand arcing out behind our wheels. Mathilda scrambled up onto the seat beside me and stood there with her forepaws braced against the windshield and giving her all to her barking.

I thought of telling her to shut up, but I knew she wasn't going to listen. In any case, I had to concentrate on my driving and I was telling myself that it would make no difference. They would see my lights come up behind them. There was no chance of taking them by surprise.

They were eating up the kilometers, but Baby was doing

better. From the moment we came up on the causeway, we'd begun gaining on them. We had to hope they weren't carrying guns or that, if they were, they wouldn't be good shots. It was riding the probabilities again. I was finding comfort in the way I had been taken out up there on the ramparts. It had been silent and skillful. It hadn't been any conk on the skull with a gun butt. I was telling myself that a man with a gun on him wouldn't have taken the chancy course of his thumb finding the precise trigger point in the dark. He would have gone for the surer thing, the gun butt to my skull. For a moment or two I drove one-handed while I was using the other for exploring my scalp. I was just verifying. I found no tender spots.

Enough of that. I brought my exploring hand down on the wheel and put away from me all thought of anything but catching up with that car that was speeding along ahead of us. It seemed the better part of forever before we came to within shooting range. It couldn't have been more than a matter of minutes, but Mathilda filled those minutes with at least a thousand barks.

As we pulled in ever closer, the possibility of shooting faded more and more. I was trying to think ahead to how I would handle it once I did catch up with them. I had no clear ideas, and first I had to catch up. Something would come to me in time. Something had to come to me.

We drew up near enough for me to see that there were two people in the car. That worried me. I could figure it for nothing but that there had been at least two of them up on the ramparts. One had made the grab on Barbie. One had dealt with me. Could it have been the same method on both of us? One man, and he first took Barbie out and, dropping her, worked on me? Then picked her up, slung her over his shoulder, and ran off with her to his car?

I couldn't make myself believe it. It came too close to being Superman stuff. So then there were the alternatives to worry about. Barbie had gone willingly. He'd had only me to deal with. I had my eyes fixed on the two people I could see in that car ahead of me. If one of them was Barbie, it had to be that she had gone willingly. Even if she was tied and gagged, wouldn't she be squirming and flinging herself about in the seat? Why would she be sitting there so still and showing no sign of struggle?

We pulled nearer and I could see that they were two men. That brought up the big question. Where was Barbie? Trussed up and flat on the rear seat or down on the floor back there? That was the best answer. It was the one I wanted to hang on to. I couldn't let myself think of the other possibilities. They could be two guys who, given that long, straight stretch of the causeway, couldn't resist testing out how fast they could make their wheels roll, a pair of innocents who unwittingly were pulling Mathilda and me off on a false trail.

Actually, they didn't have to be innocents. There was nothing to say there had been only two of them. I began thinking about three men. Two had worked the snatch up on the ramparts, and two were now leading us off down the causeway, while a third had Barbie somewhere back there waiting to sneak her out after I had been pulled far enough away.

I began sweating. I began asking Mathilda if she knew what she was doing. I turned to asking myself if I knew what I was doing. All the time we were pulling in closer and, bit by bit, we pulled alongside. Carefully I edged in, crowding them with Baby. I had to be careful. I couldn't risk running them off the causeway. If they were a pair of innocents, that would be murder. If they weren't and they had Barbie tied up and pushed down out of sight, it would again be murder and she the victim.

They were shouting at me, but all I knew of it was seeing their mouths move. Mathilda's barking was drowning them out. There was nothing for it but to go along as I was, keeping the pressure on them, waiting for their nerve to crack. I had to pray that at the cracking point they wouldn't do something crazy and kill Barbie and themselves.

We were racing along parallel, hub to hub, but then they began to slacken speed. I slowed with them, holding them in tight all the time. They pulled to a stop and sat in their car glaring at me. I jumped for them, and Mathilda jumped with me. She was over the door at her side of the car and running around behind it. The two guys sat tight. Mathilda had given up on the barking and was back to the excited whimper. Over that I could hear them.

"What's with you, mister?" one of them said. "Are you crazy or what?"

"You want to kill yourself, go ahead and welcome," the other one contributed. "You don't have no call to go taking anybody with you."

It was English, and American English at that. I was working at thinking it meant something. They knew I was American. They knew at least that much about me. Wouldn't they otherwise have been yelling at me in French? Even as I was making the try with that thought, I knew it was no good. The odds were too strong that they had no French or, even if they had some, that they couldn't come up with it in a moment of stress. It was, after all, just the kind of moment when a man yells what comes without any thought about language. I lunged for the back seat and looked in. It was empty. The floor back there was also empty.

"Where is she?" I said. "You've got her. Where is she?"

Turning away from me, they spoke to each other.

"He is crazy," the one said.

"Crazy or out of his head stoned," said the other.

Mathilda was back to her running-back-and-forth routine. She ran to me and, whining, ran back behind the car and jumped at the trunk. Then she ran back to me and did a repeat on it. I got the message.

"Come on out of there and open your trunk," I said.

"What for? Who are you to be telling us what to do?"

"I'm the guy who's going to make you do it."

If you ask me how I was planning to accomplish that, I can't say that I had any clear ideas. All I knew was that I was going to have to make them open that car trunk and, since I had to do it, I was going to do it.

"You and who else?"

It was the inevitable response, but it wasn't all that bad a question. They had me two to one. Even though, but for the lip, they were, under the circumstances, being remarkably docile, I was looking them over. They looked big and tough. Unless I was very wrong, I'd had from at least one of them a demonstration of no little effectiveness. It was no good standing there just thinking about it. Mathilda was making it clear that she expected a great deal more than that from me, and I expected no less of myself.

I wrenched the car door open and, taking a good fistful of the nearer lug's shirtfront, I hauled him out of the car. He came without fighting me.

"Now hold it, mister," he said. "We don't want to mess with you. So don't go messing with us. You'll just get yourself hurt, that's all."

"Open the trunk," I said.

He hauled back and started a swing. I think he meant it only as a threat. Nobody telegraphs a punch that plainly. I moved inside it, taking it glancingly on my shoulder, and I slapped him, the flat of my palm against one cheek, a backhander for the other. I wasn't holding back. I was rocking his head.

Meanwhile, out of the corner of my eye, I was seeing the other man scramble out of the car. He had something in his hand and he was running around the nose of the car to come up behind me. I couldn't wait for that. I let go my hold on my man's shirtfront. He jabbed for my gut and was readying a right to my jaw. Stepping back from it, I shot my own punch at him. It landed just right. He went down and out.

I had to hope he would stay out long enough for me to take care of his buddy. I swung around to meet that one. I saw what he had in his hand. It was a tire iron and he was swinging it at my head. I shot my hand up to grab it, but I didn't get to touch it. He dropped it to the road before my hand ever reached it and, yowling with pain, took off down the causeway with Mathilda in hot pursuit.

The key was in the ignition, and a second key dangled from the chain. It was just what I wanted, the key to the trunk. I grabbed it and ran around back to open the trunk. Barbie was in there, tied hand and foot and gagged. I pulled her out and untied her. As soon as I had her hands free, she took care of the gag herself.

"This does it," she said. "This is the end of him."

"End of whom?" I asked.

"Johnny Gibbs, who else?"

"I saw the other guy. He isn't Johnny."

"Of course he isn't. Mr. Gibbs never does his own dirty work, and his hired hands aren't worth a dime. He's too cheap to hire anybody competent."

"They aren't altogether incompetent," I said. "If I hadn't had Mathilda to help me, they'd have brought it off."

"Mathilda? Where is she?"

"Chasing one of the lugs down to Pontorson. I think she bit him."

"Good for Mathilda, except that I hope it doesn't poison her."

I poked the one we had with my foot. He didn't stir. I'd caught him a good, solid one, quite enough to put him out. He was staying that way too long, but there was nothing amiss with his breathing. I had a hunch that he had come around and that he was now playing possum. I tried with my foot again, giving him a harder nudge.

"This one," I said, 'isn't out any more. He's just choosing to stay down."

"Even a dope Johnny hires can smarten up that much," Barbie said.

Having picked up the tire iron, she was standing over the fallen man, hefting it.

"No," I said.

"What do you want to do with him?" she asked.

"We'll tie him up and go after Mathilda and the other man."

"No, we won't. We don't want either of these dopes."

"*We* don't," I said, "but the police will."

"The police," she said, "can do their own work. No police."

"Why? You just said you were through with Johnny."

"I am, but this is private and I want to keep it private. I don't want to have to go to court. I don't want to be all over the papers. I don't want any part of it. I want to forget him and everything about him."

"There are laws," I said.

"French laws."

She took the keys out of the trunk lock. Taking a good

windup, she flung them out to one side of the causeway. They landed somewhere off there in the sand. Then she went to the front of the car and lifted the hood. That girl knew her automobiles. One by one she took out the sparkplugs, and one by one she heaved them after the keys.

"What's that for?" I asked.

"So they won't be going anywhere for a while."

Just then Mathilda came waddling back. She jumped all over Barbie, and then she jumped all over me. I looked down at my hand where she had licked it. It was smeared with blood. Catching hold of Mathilda, I pulled her over to where Baby's headlights shone on her. She was okay. The blood was smeared on her muzzle, but it wasn't hers.

"She got in a good bite," I said.

"She's a darling," said Barbie.

I was keeping an eye on the man who was lying on the road. He couldn't be disregarded. If I was right about him and he was playing possum, he needed to be watched. It hardly seemed possible that he wouldn't be trying to pull something sudden. Then there was the other possibility, and that was also worrying. This prolonged unconsciousness could mean that I had done him more damage than I knew. Barbie might have been satisfied to leave him there to die on the road. I wasn't.

I squatted down beside him and went over him. His breathing was good. Pulse and heartbeat were steady. He'd just crumpled. He hadn't hit his head when he went down, and he'd done himself no other injury. I went through his pockets, and when I rolled him over to get at the pockets that had been out of reach, there was just a moment of resistance before he remembered that an unconscious man doesn't resist. I was satisfied that he was okay. Out where there was no hiding place, he was hiding as best he could.

He had some francs on him and some pills. He also had a few cigarettes that weren't tobacco. He had nothing on him that could serve as identification.

Barbie came up behind me.

"The hell with him," she said. "Let's go."

Taking Mathilda with her, she settled herself in Baby. I picked the man up and dumped him in the car—in their car, not in the Porsche. Although I was certain that as soon as we were away from there he would pick himself up, I couldn't feel right about leaving him lying in the road where somebody, speeding through the night, might run over him.

I climbed aboard and set Baby rolling, continuing in the direction we'd been going. I had it in mind to try to find the other man, the toothsome one Mathilda had run off. I was waiting to hear a protest from Barbie. None came. I rolled the full length of the causeway and saw no one. It was no good going any further. The guy couldn't possibly have made it that far on foot, even if he hadn't been limping on a dog-bitten leg.

At the end of the causeway I did a U-turn. Barbie reacted to that.

"What are you doing now?" she asked.

"Going back," I said.

"What for?"

"First," I said, "to look for the other guy. When he saw us coming, he went off the road and hid."

"And when he sees us coming back, he'll hide again."

"Probably," I agreed, "but we've got to try. Mathilda did a job on him. He'll need a doctor."

"That's silly. We know she isn't rabid."

"All the same, he needs a doctor and the police."

"No doctor and no police."

I tried to reason with her. If we did as she was insisting we do, we'd be leaving the thing unreported.

"What happens when they go to the police and say we attacked them and left them to die on the road? Okay, we say they attacked first. They tried to kidnap you. How much credibility are we going to have?"

"They won't go to the police."

"How can you know they won't?"

"I know they won't because I know Johnny."

Baby's lights picked up the stranded car. The hood was up and the guy we'd left there was out of the car and bent over the engine. As soon as our lights hit him, he scurried back to climb into the car. He was lying on the car seat when we went by. I could guess that he was back to pretending unconsciousness.

The other man was nowhere to be seen.

"Are you still looking for the other slob?" Barbie asked.

"No," I said. "He doesn't want to be found."

"He knows what's good for him."

"I wish you knew what's good for you," I said.

"I know."

For a girl fresh from having been snatched, trussed up, gagged, and carried off in the trunk of a car, she was sounding mighty smug. I suppose she was putting all that out of her mind while she was lapping up such satisfaction as she could from the efficiency she had shown in disabling their car.

"Does this happen to you often?" I asked.

"What do you take me for? You think I'd let him do it to me more than once?"

"I don't know what to think."

She chose to leave me not knowing.

"Aren't you going to turn around?" she asked.

"You're the one who just wanted to leave them there," I reminded her. "You didn't want to mess with them any more."

"Oh, them," she said. "Forget them. It's the hotel. We're not going back there."

"Where are we going?" I asked.

"Away from here, anywhere away from here, someplace where Johnny won't know where I am."

"And we leave the hotel holding the bill?"

"You can always send them a check. They'll have our luggage."

"Afraid of what Johnny will do next?" I asked.

"Afraid of him? That'll be the day."

"Good. Then, there's no reason for not staying put," I said. "If, come morning, the police should want us, we're going to be where they can find us. We're not going to be in the greatest shape for them as it is, but, if on top of everything, we've lammed out during the night . . . I don't know about you, but that's not for me and it's not for Mathilda. I like France and I like almost everything about it. I say 'almost' because there's one thing I'm not going to like, and that's a French slammer."

"If those dopes do go to the police, you know what's going to happen," she said.

"I know, but I see no sign that *you* do. We'll have to do some fast talking and we won't be in the best position for it. If they have to go scouring the country for us, we'll be in a worse position."

"They'll take Mathilda into quarantine. They do that to dogs, no matter who they bite."

"They do, but don't kid yourself that we can take off and they won't catch up with us. It's not that big a country, and back at the hotel they'll find all the identification on us they could possibly need."

"So we just go the hotel and wait for the *flics?*"

"We go to the hotel and leave properly in the morning."

I put Baby back in her parking space on the sands and we walked back in through the King's Gate. While we'd been busy out on the causeway, the abbey floodlighting had been turned off. There was still the moon, but not much of its light could make it down into the narrow passageway that's known as the Grande Rue. It was dark in there. Barbie stayed close to me, hanging on to my arm, and Mathilda was right at heel.

As promised, the hotel door was locked for the night. More than that, the steel shutters were up. We climbed the stone steps to the ramparts and made for that upstairs door the hotel left open for the use of its night prowlers. That was also as promised. It was unlocked. We went in and I shut it behind us. When I turned to start toward our rooms, Barbie stopped me.

"Aren't you going to lock it?" she asked.

"And lock out some hotel guest who's having a late night?"

"He can have a later night. Lock it, Matt."

Instead of trying to give her an argument, I turned back. I wasn't worrying any, because I knew that door. It had no lock. I could think of no easier way to handle her at that moment than by giving her a demonstration. She took it hard.

"You mean just anybody can walk in here and take us while we're asleep?"

"I thought you weren't afraid."

"I won't shut my eyes all night."

She did shut her eyes. It took time because first we had to wash the blood off Mathilda and then, when I kissed her good night and made as if to head for that separate room she'd insisted on, she wasn't insisting any more. She held me, and what had begun as a good-night kiss became something different. It was a beginning.

"Don't go, Matt," she said. "With that unlocked door out there, I won't feel safe unless you're with me. Stay, Matt. Please."

She did say "please," didn't she? Where's there a man who can refuse a request like that, especially when the girl asks so nicely and politely.

I could have reminded her that it was a single room and there was only the one single bed in it, but what could that do except put some idea into her head, like maybe she could suggest that Erridge sleep on the floor? I said nothing. I was thinking about that unlocked door. It seemed to me that it was a hotel amenity that should catch on the world over. It just didn't seem right that hotels everywhere shouldn't be offering their guests something that useful.

Mathilda slept on the floor, but only until we had drifted off to sleep. Sometime after that she joined us. When we woke the next morning, we were three in the bed. It couldn't have been more cozy.

I called down and ordered breakfast. They sent up three. Ours was great. I don't know what there was in Mathilda's but she slurped it up with manifest enjoyment. That late snack of malefactor's leg she had taken the night before hadn't spoiled her appetite.

While I'd been on the phone putting in the breakfast order, Barbie had broken out some Michelin Green Guides. She had them for Normandy and Brittany. All through breakfast she divided herself between eating and reading. A copy of that morning's *Figaro* had come up with the breakfast trays. I flipped that while she busied herself with the Green Guides. There wasn't much in the paper, mostly the standard run of French political infighting. There was a cartoon of Liberty holding the Concorde at arm's length while she stood hip deep in a rock band of about symphony orchestra size. I was looking for local news even though I was telling myself it was too soon. Even if those guys we'd left out on the causeway had gone to the police, there wouldn't have been time for any word of it to have made this edition of *Figaro*. It also seemed to me that, well before any story could have hit the paper, the flics would have come down on Barbie and me, not to speak of Mathilda. We'd had no flics and, what with it having been a crowded night followed by more love before breakfast, we were having a late morning.

The nearest thing to a local story I came on was one about the truck farmers in Brittany. They were up in arms about what Common Market pricing had done to the price of cabbages. They were threatening a farmers' strike.

Barbie looked up from her guidebooks.

"Where do we go from here?" she asked.

"Where do you want to go? Back to Dinard?"

"Anyplace *but*. I suppose I'll have to go back there sometime to pick up my stuff, but that can wait, or maybe I'll just leave it. One of the hotel maids can pack it up and send it on to me. Now I want to go everywhere and see everything. Will you take me, Matt? You hate Dinard. You know you do."

"Dinard bores me," I said.

I had been about to add that I did have my man back there, but I let that go by. There was no point to it. I could phone and check in with him, but that would only be to tell him where he could reach me. He wasn't going to be wanting me now. It had only been overnight.

Barbie launched into a long recital.

"I want to see Coutances and Lessay and Bayeux and Caen," she said. "I want to go to Falaise and see the castle where that bastard, William, was born. You're right. He really was a bastard. It says here that Robert had the beautiful Arletta to love. It doesn't say anywhere that he ever married her."

"He didn't," I said. "Up to 1066 when he crossed the Channel and took England, he was known as William the Bastard. It was only after the Battle of Hastings that anybody called him William the Conqueror."

"It must have been a nice change for him, the louse. It says here at Bayeux you can see in the tapestry where Harold came here with him and saved him from the quicksands. Why didn't the dope just leave him to be sucked in?"

"Maybe by 1066 Harold was asking himself the same question," I said.

I was thinking something else. In the time she'd been between bites and sips, the girl had been a quick study. She'd mapped out an extensive tour of major sites of Romanesque Normandy. I had to think that she had been doing some earlier preparation. Coming here to Mont St. Michel had only been the entering wedge. From the first, I was thinking, she'd had plans for sucking me into the rest of this. I would have liked to believe that inside that beautiful head there lived a serious-minded history-and-Romanesque-art buff and that she went for the kind of guiding Erridge provided.

"The babe is playing you, Erridge," I was telling myself.

Myself talked right back at me.

"Last night was nice," it told me. "This morning's been nice. Other nights, other mornings, great days in between. Are we the man who'd want to fight it?"

III.

We weren't.

We dressed. We packed up. I checked us out properly and we took off down the causeway. By that time it was well into the morning. The buses and the day trippers were there in full force, and more of them were pouring in. For us the traffic was light. The heavy stream was going the other way, in toward the Mont. I watched for the disabled car, but of course it wasn't there. It was most unlikely that it would be. Even if those guys had been stuck all through the night, first thing in the morning the *flics* would have come on them and towed them away. They wouldn't leave anything on the causeway to obstruct traffic.

Maybe the French police do other things as well, but one thing I know they don't neglect. It is only when they are confronted with the totally impossible, like a Paris boulevard barricaded with ripped-up cobblestones and chopped-down trees, that they fail to keep the traffic moving. One stranded set of wheels would be no problem for them. They've too often been confronted with worse.

We set forth on Barbie's route. It was Coutances and Lessay. In both places Barbie tried hard, but I could sense that she was trying. She had asked for them, but neither the stupendous towers of Coutances nor the great piers and vaults of Lessay seemed to get through to her. She was clearly occupied with thoughts she wasn't sharing with me. For a while there, Mathilda was better company. After Lessay, however, on the drive across the base of the Cotentin peninsula Barbie shook off that mood, whatever it was. She worked at being gay and animated. I had an uneasy feeling that perhaps it wasn't there. It was just something she was working at, but she was doing such a good job of it that before long it seemed genuine. I wasn't going to question it. It was more fun just riding along with it.

There were a couple of questions, though, that I did have sitting in my mind. Nothing she had done when we were leaving Dinard had carried any suggestion that she might have told Ken-Johnny that she was taking off with me and that I was going to show her Mont St. Michel. So what about the kidnap attempt? When he'd wanted to send his muscle out after her, he'd known where to find her. So now she had come up with the rest of the route, far more of it than she could possibly have mapped out on nothing more than those quick dips into the guides over breakfast. Was he sitting back there in Dinard with this whole itinerary in hand making his decisions on just when and where we were to be intercepted?

The more I thought about it, the more I came to feel that she owed me a little clarification.

"When do we hear from Johnny next?" I asked.

"We won't."

"You were wrong once," I told her. "You said he wouldn't care. You said he wouldn't even know you were gone. He not only knew you were gone. He knew *where* as well."

"I've been thinking about that," she said.

I hadn't been going to ask her about her mood, but now I was doing it.

"Is that what you had on your mind?" I asked. "Back there in Coutances and on into Lessay you had something on your mind."

She nodded.

"That was it," she said. "There was no way he could have known where to find me last night, and yet his goons did find me. There's only one way they could have done it."

"And that is?"

"He has spies," she said. "I knew all along he had spies. I suppose I should have known he'd have them in that Dinard hotel. It must have been a chambermaid. She tells him I'm packing up, so he has those idiots waiting outside the hotel, and they followed us. It couldn't have been any other way. I got to thinking that maybe they'd be following us again today. That's what I was doing before, watching to see if we were being followed."

"Were we? Are we?"

"No. Of course not. It was silly even to think it. How could they be following? You saw how scared they were by the time we got through with them, and that isn't all—there's the way I left their car. Sure, they got a tow and any garage could put new plugs in for them, but there was the car key. Where I threw it, do you think they could ever find it?"

"They could have had a spare," I said. "Of course, if they had to wait for a replacement, it would have taken time and then they would have been too late to follow us today, but there's also another thing they could have done."

"Like what?"

"Like picking up another car. You can get a car hire practically anywhere these days," I said.

She scowled.

"I didn't think of that."

"There's nothing following us now."

"And there wasn't before. I was watching."

"Watching for their car or for any car?" I asked.

"For their car, I guess," she said. "But if it had been another car, I'd have noticed. There hasn't been any car."

"You asked him to take you to Mont St. Michel and he wouldn't . . ." I began.

"I told you that," she said.

"Did you talk about all these other places you wanted to go to and all the other things you wanted to see? Lessay, Coutances, Bayeux, Caen, Falaise? The whole route or any part of it?"

"No," she said. "I didn't because I couldn't have. I only just read about them this morning at breakfast. Back in Dinard I didn't even know they were around or anything about them."

"You knew Mont St. Michel was around," I reminded her. "You knew about it."

"Oh, that. Who doesn't? Everybody knows about that. You saw yourself how it was. Everybody and his uncle was swarming all over the place, but today Coutances and Lessay, nobody knows about them. You saw how we had them to ourselves."

She was lying and I knew it. I'd been there. I'd seen how little time she'd had with those Michelin guides. Also, what she was saying about Coutances and Lessay might have been true enough, but Bayeux would not be another place we would have to ourselves. You could hardly have gone to school, at least not in England or America, without having heard of the Bayeux tapestry. Maybe she had never known of it till she had come on it in the guidebook at breakfast, but I was finding that hard to believe. On the little I'd seen of him, I could think her Johnny-Ken had never heard of it, but I wasn't ready to say he wouldn't have heard of it from her.

We lunched in Bayeux, and after lunch I showed her the

cathedral and the tapestry. It's a busy town, but it was quiet in the cathedral. The room where they have the tapestry was jammed, but only with bands of school kids and the occasional harried adult who had them in tow, nobody who looked even remotely like the two guys we'd left on the causeway.

We moved on to Caen for the night, and now she was insisting on a double room for the three of us. I offered no resistance. I called Dinard to check in with Elston. I got through to his number, but he wasn't there. The man who answered took the message. If Elston wanted to reach me, I was going to be at the hotel in Caen for a couple of nights.

"Where are you going after that?" the guy asked.

"I don't know," I said. "Why?"

"When Mr. Elston wants to reach you, he'll want to get through to you right off," the man said. "Just give me your itinerary, and then you won't have to call us. We'll call you."

I told him I didn't know where I'd be next. So we left it that I'd call him before leaving Caen and fill him in on the next stop. Barbie seemed to be hanging on every word of my end of that phone call. There was no telling what was going to interest that girl. The phone conversation could hardly have been duller.

"Your man keeps you on a leash," she said when I'd hung up. "It may be a long leash, but it's there when he wants to pull you in."

I shrugged it off.

"He couldn't care less," I said. "One of his boys is out to make himself some good marks for efficiency. He would like to tell the boss more than the boss wants to know."

We did the two great abbey churches and the Bastard-Conqueror's castle. We ate tripe. At least Mathilda and I ate it. Barbie didn't like hers. She passed it on to Mathilda and I ordered her something else. Mathilda lapped it up.

We drove out into the country and I took her down to Falaise. That's a big castle down there and Barbie loved it. She had a ball standing at the window they say is the one from which young Robert looked out day after day, keeping his eye on the spring down below where the beautiful Arletta came to do her laundry. With her skirt tucked up around her waist while she scrubbed her clothes, she built that overwhelming yen in seventeen-year-old Robert, the yen that resulted in William.

When you look out now, you don't see any spring. There's a swimming pool down there instead, so the view is no worse than it was back in 1027. On the return trip up to Caen, Barbie had her guidebooks out. She studied them as I drove. That night over dinner she fed me the results of her reading.

"Where do we go next?" she asked.

"Where do you want to go?"

"Anyplace I like, Matt? Can we? All the places I want to see? I want to see them with you."

"Anyplace you like," I said.

I did think that I should have added "within reason," but the days had been good and the nights had been great, and I wasn't about to let reason spoil the fun.

It was all she needed. She had done her homework.

"For starters," she said, "Les Andelys."

Maybe she was hooked on castles, and maybe she had caught on to how much I'm hooked on the engineering feats of those eleventh- and twelfth-century buckos. The Château Gaillard down there is an even bigger one than Falaise and a great one. It was Richard the Lion Heart's baby, and John Lackland lost it. It sits in a great piece of country.

"Okay," I said, "Les Andelys."

I called Elston, but again I got only the secretary. I knew of a not bad hotel in Vernon, and from Les Andelys that's only about fifteen miles up the Seine. I told him we'd be there the following night. It wasn't enough. He wanted more.

"Where will you be all day?"

"On the road."

"I know that," he said. "Give me your route."

"What for?"

"If he wants to talk to you during the day."

"He'll wait till evening," I said. "How can he talk to me while I'm driving?"

He told me how. If the secretary knew my route, he could get through to the police in the towns I'd be hitting on the way. He'd give them my license number and they'd catch me with Elston's message as I came by. Then, wherever I was, I could stop and call back.

Of course it could be done, and for the Elstons of this world it might seem a reasonable enough way to operate. The police, after all, are public servants. So whom should they serve if not the inordinately rich?

"That urgent?" I asked.

"When Mr. Elston wants something, he wants it immediately."

I promised myself that when Mr. Elston got around to wanting Erridge, he wasn't going to have him anything like immediately. I was thinking of what Barbie had said about the leash, and I was coming down with a feeling that she might have been reading it right. One tug on the leash and Erridge comes running back to Dinard? I would map it out when the time came, but when it came, it was going to be by a leisurely and circuitous route.

"You're crazy," I said, "but if you want it, okay."

I lined it out for him: Pont-l'Évêque, Pont-Audemer, then skirting south of Rouen, Louviers, Les Andelys, and Vernon.

We hit the road in the morning and loafed along the way, taking detours off the highway now and again for places I wanted to show her en route. I don't know how much it was that I wanted her to see these places and how much the diversions from the route I'd given Elston's secretary were done for myself. They gave me reassurance. They told me I was still my own man.

It was late afternoon when we came into Les Andelys. The Lion Heart's great fortress stands on a high bluff overlooking the Seine and, even in ruin, looks impregnable. You can park down in the town and climb the steep footpath that zigzags up the face of the bluff, or you can drive through the town and go up by the road to come on it the way the King of France did when he took it back in 1204. He knocked off the strongpoint outside the moat and then infiltrated the main fortress through the latrines. Those latrines are long gone. You park at the foot of the fortress wall and follow a footpath through a great tract of wild park into the castle ruin.

We hadn't gone far along the path before Mathilda left us. There were rabbits to chase. I congratulated myself on my timing. We were going to be seeing it in the sunset light when the marks of ruin are lost in the shadows and the river down below gleams with sunset fire. From time to time Mathilda came running back to check in with us, but then she would be off again after the rabbits.

We were ready to go back down, but first we climbed up onto the ramparts to watch from there when the horizon sucked in the sun. It was a great moment and we were having it all to ourselves. The castle gets its share of day trippers. Those woods over which it sits are perfect for picnics, but, come sundown, the buses have pulled out and the cars have all hit the road for Evreux or up the river to Paris. We could look down into the parking area. Baby stood there alone.

The shot whistled past my ear. I knew the sound: No man who's ever been under sniper fire will forget that air-ripping whistle. Grabbing Barbie, I pulled her down behind the parapet and fell on top of her. She laughed.

"No, Matt," she said. "Not now. Not here."

"Stay down."

"Don't be ridiculous," she said. "There's a sharp stone and it's biting into my back. Let's at least go down on the grass. That stone hurts."

"All right," I said. "Roll away from it, but stay down."

"What's gotten into you?"

"You didn't hear it? It was a rifle shot. We're under fire, kid."

She didn't believe me, or she was pretending not to.

"The King of France?" she giggled.

"Your Johnny," I said. "Isn't it nice to be wanted that much?"

"That's insane. There's been nobody since that first day. How could they know we were here?"

It was a good question, but it seemed to me that if either of us knew the answer, it wouldn't be Erridge.

"Suppose you tell me," I said.

"You're the one who's saying they're here," she argued. "Just because it happened that night up on a parapet, you're getting ideas about parapets. You're imagining things."

"Baby," I said, "I can imagine a lot of things, but I don't imagine rifle slugs."

I started up. She moved under me. I thought she was just rolling away from her sharp stone, but she was trying to get up with me. I had to push her back down. Holding her there with one hand, I heaved myself up, bringing my head up for a split second. The response was immediate. A slug whammed into the parapet, knocking stone chips out of the weathered masonry. The shattered bits pattered down around us.

Her eyes widened.

"That was a shot? It was meant for you?"

She wasn't asking me. She was putting her questions more to herself. The second shot had forced her into belief. She was trying to come to terms with it.

"Stay where you are," I told her. "And stay down. Don't follow me."

She grabbed hold of me.

"Where are you going?"

"I'll try to spot them," I said.

"You'll get your head shot off."

"Not today I won't. I know what I'm doing."

"That last one came close. They won't miss every time."

"They'll miss every time. I'm going to make them miss."

"You're sure you know what you're doing?"

"I'm sure."

Holding myself down in a crouch, I moved off along the ramparts. I had chosen my direction, moving toward the steps we had mounted to get up there. There was no other means of access. The French King's men had infiltrated through the latrines. If these buckos should try to infiltrate, I had to keep myself between them and Barbie.

After I'd put about twenty-five feet between myself and the girl, I put my head up for a look around. I could see nothing. Baby stood alone in the parking lot. Otherwise, it was only trees and shrubbery, the road up, the tangles of undergrowth that flanked the road, and way down below the sunset-reddened river.

I didn't stay up there long. Pulling back down, I moved on another five or six feet and tried again. This time I caught a bright flash. It could have been the light of the lowering sun reflected off a rifle barrel. They were down there, well concealed in the underbrush. They had chosen their position well. They were between us and Baby. That long time ago when Philip Augustus had taken the place, he had spent a year and more besieging it before he attacked. I wondered if they had come prepared for a long siege.

Bobbing up and down, I tried to see more. After a few minutes of that, I began to wonder why I wasn't drawing fire. Then I looked back to see what Barbie was doing. The idiot was on her feet and was standing there looking down, offering herself as an easy, stationary target.

I shouted to her to get down, but she didn't move. I forgot about keeping it low and made a dash for her. A quick shot, zinging past me, reminded me. I hauled myself down and ran in a crouch. I grabbed her and pulled her down.

"What do you think you're doing?" I asked.

"Looking for them," she said. "They're down there in the bushes."

"I know where they are. You could have gotten yourself shot."

"No, I couldn't. He wants me back, but it wouldn't be dead or alive. They won't shoot at me. They're only shooting at you."

She had a point. I had to admit that she had demonstrated it. She was all for giving me another demonstration, but I told her I was convinced.

"Stay down anyhow," I said. "They just could mistake you for me."

"We don't look alike," she said.

"The light's getting bad," I said. "It's good enough for shooting, but it's getting bad for picking targets."

"You stay here out of sight," she said. "I'll get them off you."

"And how do you think you're going to do that?"

"The only way," she said. "The obvious way. It's been nice, Matt, and thanks for everything, but now the party's over. I'll just go down there and go back to Dinard with them. Once I've done that, they'll have no more interest in you."

"Over my dead body," I said.

"That's just the point. I have to go back no matter what, and I don't want it to be over your dead body."

"You want to go back to him?"

"You know I don't."

"Then that's that," I said. "If you ever change your mind and you do want to go back to him, you'll go, but not this way. You'll go with me. I'll take you back to him. I'm not hiding up here while they take you away from me."

"What possible difference can it make?" she asked.

"Maybe it's a difference you can't understand, but you've got to believe me. There is a difference. You can call it pride."

"That's just a lot of *macho* nonsense," she said.

"One of my problems, baby. I thought you'd have noticed. I'm stuffed full of macho nonsense."

"All right, then. Have you any ideas?"

"I'm full of ideas. You just stay down out of sight and let me handle this."

"And what if you get yourself killed?"

"I've never done that and I'm not starting now."

"There's always a first time for everything, and when it's getting killed, the first is also the last."

"That," I said, "is so logical, you ought to be French."

"I have to know what you're going to do," she insisted.

"Why?"

"It's only fair. *I* told *you.*"

"You *had* to tell me. You needed my co-operation. All I need is for you to stay down out of sight."

"While we're arguing," she said, "they're probably on their way up here, coming in after you."

"I'll test that out," I said.

I bobbed up and right back down again. The shot knocked some more chips off the parapet.

"See?" she said.

"It says they're still down there, right where they were."

"You're going to do that one time too many."

"Just enough," I said, "not too much."

"You're crazy."

"This is going to look crazy, but trust me, kid. I like being alive."

The trick of moving along the parapet and bobbing up in a place they weren't expecting wasn't going to work as well as it had. Showing my head while I was running back to Barbie had tipped them off to that one. They were going to be looking for it now. I was facing up to that, but it wasn't worrying me. Whatever the fix you're in, you have to take the situation as it stands and try to turn it to your advantage.

I scuttled along about ten feet and then put my head up. I didn't leave it up for any measurable time and I drew no shot. Up again, I held it just a fraction longer. That time the shot came, but it was wide. I had all I needed to know. Zeroed in on the spot where they had seen me with Barbie, they could react quickly and with reasonable accuracy. Shooting at me wherever I might bob up, they took a tick longer to get on target and their accuracy went off.

Scurrying back and forth and bobbing up here and there,

I kept drawing their fire. I had them firing steadily and spraying rifle slugs over a wide area. I had no way of knowing how much of that it would take to run them out of ammo, but I wasn't counting on that. It was a warm, dry night. At the worst we could stay up on the parapet till morning brought the next day's invading busloads of day trippers. Time was on my side, but there was the hotel down in Vernon and there was dinner and there was bed. I was hoping for something better than a night on the hard stone of the Lion Heart's battlements.

After a few minutes of this, I had to stop to catch my breath. I moved back to check on how Barbie was doing. She was sitting on the stone, properly down out of sight, and she had Mathilda stretched across her lap. The pup had the shakes, something like jello mounted on a pogo stick.

"I hope you're having fun, you idiot," Barbie said. "All that gunfire has Mathilda scared silly."

"When we're out of this," I promised, "I'll find a way to make it up to her."

I couldn't spend more than a few moments with them. The light was going fast and my remaining chance to draw more fire would be going with it. I went back to my scurrying and bobbing game.

Then I heard it: the sound of the siren as it raced through the town at the foot of the cliff. They heard it too. I had evidence of that when I next put my head up. I drew no fire.

But then the siren wail cut off and, when I bobbed up again, I drew another shot. That one was ridiculously wide. The sun was down and the oncoming dark had deepened past any possibility of hunting. I waited about a minute before I again offered them my head. I was still being careful. Even in the failing light my sniper could get lucky. I was up for only a moment, but in that moment I'd seen something I'd been hoping for. Through the trees I caught flickers of the glare of headlights. A car was coming up the road.

It figured. The fusillade I'd been working on drawing from my sniper down below had been heard in the town. The police were coming up to investigate. Through the narrow streets of the town they had ridden with the siren, but on the open road they weren't advertising their approach. I bobbed up for another look. The car was rolling along the road to the parking area. It passed the stretch where in the undergrowth I'd caught the light flash off the rifle barrel and it rolled on, heading straight for Baby. There was no need to get down again. Now I could watch.

After the police car had passed, another car emerged from behind a clump of trees and bumped onto the road. Quickly it picked up speed and whizzed off toward the town down below. Our friends weren't waiting for the flics to double back and find them.

I walked back to Barbie. She was screaming at me.

"Get down, you fool. They'll kill you."

"Not this time," I said. "You can stand up now. The show's over. They're gone."

She stood up and looked over the parapet.

"There's a car down there," she said. "They've moved to the parking lot. They're waiting for us there."

"That's the police," I told her. "All that shooting up here. It's not like it was hunting season."

She laughed.

"That's what you were doing," she said. "Making them shoot so the police would come."

I laughed with her.

"That's what I was doing," I said. "We can go down now."

She shook her head.

"Let's wait till the police are gone," she said.

"They won't go. They've found the Porsche. They know we're up here. They'll be beating the bushes for us. As it is, we haven't a very good story to tell them, since we didn't report the thing back there at Mont St. Michel. It's not going to improve our credibility if we make ourselves hard to find. We're going to them. We're not waiting for them to come to us."

I took her arm to guide her toward the steps. The dark was closing in. It was going to be difficult to watch the footing.

"We're not telling them anything," she said.

"Why not?"

"I told you the other time."

"That's silly."

"So I'm silly."

"We can't pretend we didn't hear the shooting."

"We heard it and we saw some boys shooting at rabbits."

"I'm no rabbit and I don't like being mistaken for one."

She stopped and kissed me.

"You're wonderful," she said, "and you're a darling."

"Flattery," I said.

"Boys and rabbits," she begged. "For me, Matt."

"You know what I am going to do for you," I said. "One of these days I'm going to catch up with your Ken-Johnny and I'm going to take him apart. Whether you're going to want to put him together again will be up to you."

"I'm through with him," she said. "I don't want ever to see him again. It's not for him, Matt. It's for me."

We went on down through the castle ruin, and just before we came out on to the road we ran into the flics.

They were scowling. At the corner of the mustache one

of them was sporting I could see a fleck of something. It looked like Sauce Béchamel. They had been taken away from their dinner. They were feeling ugly.

Barbie gave with the cheery "*Bon soir.*"

They were seeing nothing good about the evening. They growled about the *chasse*, hunting licenses, the season.

Barbie came back with *garçon* and *lapin*. They showed no symptoms of being convinced. They held us and they patted us down. They took us down to the Porsche and did a search of Baby. I was tempted to tell them that Barbie was a liar, but there were all sorts of things holding me back. It was late for telling them about the kidnap attempt. Barbie was out on a limb. I couldn't bring myself to chop her off.

Also, it was dinnertime. The flics were obviously being stern with themselves and doing their job, even though they wanted very much to return to their unfinished meal. If I opened that can of worms, they'd never get back to it and we'd never get to the dinner we had waiting for us up the river at Vernon. My stomach was yelling at me, it was dinnertime. It was long past time for a drink.

All those things were factors, but the main event was Barbie. I've said the girl was out on a limb, but I'd come down with some fresh ideas of how far out. I could see no possible way that those men could have known we were going to explore the Château Gaillard that afternoon unless she had passed them the word.

This baby was playing games. I didn't know just what the games were, and I was promising myself that sooner or later I was going to find out, but that wasn't the same as tossing her to the flics and leaving it to them to find out for me.

I backed her up on the garçon and lapin story. Their search of Baby was giving them nothing. We'd been clean and Baby was clean. No rifles. No ammo. Not so much as a cap pistol.

So then they wanted to know what we'd been doing up there after dark.

"We'd been watching the sunset," I said.

They came up with the exact time the sun had gone down. They had it, hour and minute.

Barbie fielded that one.

"The moon would be coming up," she said. "It can't be that you don't have girls. Fine-looking, big, strong men like you, you must have girls. A man, a girl, the moon. You don't know?"

The gendarmes went back to their dinner. We took ourselves off to ours.

IV.

That evening I tried questioning her, but I can't say I made a good job of it. It wasn't that I lacked for questions. My head was full of them, but none of them was very much good. My trouble was that there was no way I could make any sense of what was going on. If I took the two episodes just for themselves, separating them from the way she had reacted to them, I could figure it that her man wanted her back and that he had rough ways of going about getting her back. That still left the question of how he could have known we would be coming to the Château Gaillard and that his men could catch up with us there.

I didn't suggest to her that she had been keeping in touch with him and briefing him on our plans and our movements, though that did seem the most reasonable explanation. It's not unknown for a woman to enjoy having guys fight over her. Let's say she wanted her fun, but she didn't want it to get out of hand. She didn't want anyone killed. That way, I could think that the first try hadn't suited her at all. Sending the two goons to kidnap her and bring her back to him could have been read for a measure of his ardor, but I could see where she might have felt it wasn't good enough. She wanted him to come after her himself. Certainly the way she had fixed their car out there on the causeway could have been strong signals to her Johnny that she was no gal to settle for second best.

One thing that had struck me from the first was that she

was too quick a study with those guidebooks. I was pretty certain that she'd had this tour of ours all planned out beforehand. If she had planned it and had put it up to Johnny and then turned to me when he refused to take her, he could have remembered and could be gambling that we were following the itinerary. It even seemed possible that he was sitting back there in Dinard with the itinerary spread out before him. That made better sense than thinking she'd been making daily phone calls to tell him where he could find us.

"I'm having a ball, old buddy. I'm going to all the places you wouldn't take me. Tomorrow we'll be at Les Andelys, and how do you like that? Matt refuses me nothing. You want me back? Well, suppose you try coming to get me. If you were any kind of man, that's what you'd do."

Something like that? It was possible, but the other seemed more likely.

I asked her if, when she was asking Johnny to take her places, she'd ever mentioned wanting to see Richard's castle.

"How could I, Matt? I'd never even heard of the place till I read about it in the guidebook."

"I thought maybe you'd been planning a trip like this and you'd been working on him to take you," I said.

"To Mont St. Michel, just one day to Mont St. Michel," she said. "I thought I could ask that much of him."

I shook my head.

"There has to be some way he could have known where we would be this afternoon," I said.

She had some questions to throw back at me.

"Today," she said. "Did you see them?"

"I didn't see anybody. I saw the glint of a rifle barrel in the bushes, and I saw the car when it took off after the police had gone by. That's all."

"The car? Was it the same one?"

"Can't say. I couldn't see the license plate. It was the same make and same model, but France is full of Citroëns."

We went round and round about it and we got nowhere. In the morning she said she was tired. She needed more sleep. Other mornings we'd both been up to take Mathilda out for a good run before breakfast. Would I mind awfully if I had to take Mathilda out alone while she caught herself another half hour of shuteye?

I didn't mind. Mathilda wanted out and Barbie wasn't stirring. She was looking tired and strained, and I was for a good, fast walk. I took off with Mathilda and did better than Barbie had asked. We stayed out for all of an hour, letting the kid catch up on her rest. When we came back, Barbie was awake and she had her nose in the guidebooks.

Over breakfast she opened it up.

"Where do we go next?" she asked.

I laughed at her.

"You've been doing your homework," I said. "Tell me."

"I've been reading about Brittany," she said. "Let's go back there."

"Dinard? Ken-Johnny?"

She kicked me.

"You know better than that," she said. "No, not there. I've been there."

"Okay. Where?"

"We've been doing all this sightseeing," she said. "I was thinking we could be lazy on some lovely beach for a day or two."

"That's Dinard again."

"It doesn't have to be Dinard. There are lots of other places nowhere near Dinard."

She'd done a good job on the homework.

"Quiberon," I suggested. "That's on the west coast, clear away from Dinard. You'll like it there."

She wrinkled her nose.

"That's near Carnac with all that Druid stuff, dolmens and menhirs, and what not. Druids give me the creeps."

"Then you've been there?"

"No. I've been reading the guidebook and it sounds creepy. There's a place that sounds much nicer. It's on the north coast but nowhere near Dinard."

"What's it called?"

"Perros-Guirec. Do you know it?"

"I've been there. Good beach, plenty of hotels, and a restaurant I like not too far away."

"Then why not, Matt?"

"I'm just wondering why, of all the places, you picked Perros-Guirec?"

"It sounds nice in the guidebook, and up that way we can see something that sounds terrific."

"I thought you'd said you'd had enough sightseeing."

"Yes, but just this. It sounds like much more fun than your old Druids."

"All right. What and where?"

"It's a little place called Guimiliau."

"Never heard of it."

She grinned.

"Good," she said. "Then I can show it to you."

"What's there?"

"The guide says a calvary in the parish close."

"What fun," I said. "A calvary sounds real cheery."

"This is a big one and it's got the story of Catell-Gollet. They also call her Catherine."

"Ought I know her?"

"*I'm* the one who should know her. She's a warning to girls against flirting."

"Isn't it too late for you?" I asked.

"I can always reform."

"I don't think I want you reformed," I said. "You could be boring."

"Not completely reformed," she promised. "Just cured of flirting. After all, you don't want me to go around flirting with other men. It's not as though I'd reformed before I flirted with you."

"As I remember it," I said, "you didn't flirt with me. Mathilda did."

"Then, maybe it'll be a lesson to her, cure her of flirting."

"Who was this Catherine and what's she doing flirting on a calvary?"

"On the calvary she's going to hell."

"Some people will tell you it's the same thing."

"That's just what her story does say," Barbie assured me.

She ran through it, telling me what she'd read in the guide. This Catherine was a servant girl and she had a thing with a guy. Barbie said the guide wasn't clear on whether the guy was the Devil, or if the Devil didn't get into the act until later when he appeared to her in the form of the guy.

What seems to have gotten her into trouble is that she went to confession and didn't confess to having been bad. That's the start of her slide down to hell. The Devil sucks her into stealing the consecrated Host off the altar for him, and that does it. She comes up on this calvary in the jaws of hell, with devils clawing chunks out of her body.

"And you're not going to be happy until you've seen that?" I asked.

"Don't you want to see if it will cure Mathilda of flirting?"

"You've drawn the wrong moral," I told her. "The way you tell it, the thing is a warning to girls to stay away from any guy who can't buy his own cookies."

"That came later," Barbie argued. "What started her downfall was having a roll with that guy, who may or may not have been the Devil."

"Okay," I said. "We'll drop in on Guimiliau if you think it's going to do Mathilda that much good."

I broke out the road map and plotted the course. We were in the process of checking out of the hotel when the call came through for me. I assumed it would be my fat cat come around to tugging at the leash. I was of a mood to keep him waiting, and only in part, because I'd promised Barbie Perros-Guirec and the mouth of hell. The guy evidently had the notion that he had only to snap his fingers and Erridge would jump. He was going to have to be disabused of that before we could have any kind of business relationship—if we were ever to have one at all. Erridge has his skills up for sale. He's not sitting on any display counter to be picked up body and soul.

It was the secretary again, but that much I had expected. You know the Mr.-Elston-calling-please-hold-on routine. You wait. He doesn't. Contrary to my expectations, however, it was nothing like that. It was just more of the same. The secretary again wanted my further itinerary just in case the great man should take a sudden fancy to get in touch. I reeled it off for him: Évreux, Alencon, Fougères, Rennes, Lamballe, St. Brieuc, Guingamp, Perros-Guirec."

"When will you be leaving?" the secretary asked.

"Right now. If you had called a minute later, you wouldn't have caught me. I was heading for the car when your call came through."

"Without letting us know where you were going to be?"

It was a yelp of pain and outrage.

"That's right," I said. "Without asking permission."

The response to that was huffy.

"You have no reason to take that tone with us, Mr. Erridge. You do want to talk with Mr. Elston, don't you?"

"Less and less," I said. "All the time less and less."

It seemed as good an exit line as any. I hung up. There was nothing but sputtering coming over the line anyway. We pulled out before he could make another call and, as we took the road down to Évreux, I was promising myself that if along the way the flics did intercept us with a message, I was not going to leap to the nearest phone. Mr. Elston was going to wait until Barbie and I'd had all we wanted of the beach at Perros-Guirec. If she did some more homework then and came up with more places she wanted me to take her, he might even have to wait longer. I had come to think that I didn't want to work for the guy. In any case, this was a fat cat who was going to need a lot of conditioning before I'd ever agree to work for him.

Those French roads are good. The country is great, and just a little ten-mile detour out of Rennes I knew a place where they'd give us a gâteau de homard for lunch. It should have been a fine day and it was. I drove along and I was comfortably relaxed. The relaxation didn't go all the way. I'm not pretending I was as relaxed as a rug, or anything near it, but beyond keeping a watchful eye out for a car I might recognize, I was enjoying the drive and the company.

The way I was figuring it, reading license numbers on cars we passed or cars that passed us was almost certainly an unnecessary precaution. Barbie's Ken-Johnny might have known we would be going to Perros-Guirec. There was no way he could have known the road I was taking to get there. There was, after all, a pattern to this thing. When trouble had come at us, it had neither time been along the road. On both occasions it had been at planned stops and never at a stop I'd thrown in along the way, only at places Barbie had asked for.

I wasn't reading all the numbers, only those on cars of the right make, model, and color. Since make, model, and color were none of them unusual, I did see some license numbers I bothered to read. None of them was the number I'd tucked away in my head that night at Mont St. Michel.

We zipped along because Baby likes to move and I like the feel of her when she's moving, but we also made stops. There was a long and leisurely lunch. Who hurries lobster? There was a pause at Fougères for a look at the castle, and another at Lamballe because it's a pretty town and Marie Antoinette's best buddy came from there.

It was after Lamballe that Barbie came up with the suggestion that we should go on past St. Brieuc for the short run to Guimiliau before heading into Perros-Guirec. She was looking at the road map and she had it all taped out. Guimiliau lay only a short jog to the south of the St. Brieuc-Morlaix highway. From Guimiliau we could hit straight for Guingamp and on up, or we could go up through Morlaix. Guimilau was practically on our way.

I'd been thinking that one of the days while we were at Perros-Guirec we'd take time out from the beach and do a run down there to have a look at the bad girl on her way to hell, but I could see no reason to be inflexible about it. We could do it Barbie's way just as comfortably, and it would be like the detour we'd taken for lunch, thumbing our nose a bit at Elston and his damn secretary.

"Afraid that hell will swallow the chick up before we get to her?" I asked.

"Afraid that once we get to the beach, we won't want to leave it," Barbie said.

"No character?"

"Me?" she said. "None at all, and I haven't noticed you have any either."

"That's what you like about me," I told her. "You twist me around your little finger."

"Poof," she said. "You're a lot better in other positions."

She was given to saying things like that, reminders that night would be coming, as though I needed any reminding with her in the car beside me.

We rolled on to the St. Brieuc bypass and had just come to the place where the highway forked. To the right it would be Guingamp and on up to the beach. Straight ahead would be Morlaix, and somewhere along that road the turnoff for Guimiliau. It was there that I saw the car. I was roaring along behind it and I read the license number. The car had its signal blinker going. It was about to take the fork up to Guingamp, but at the last minute the driver changed his mind. Despite what his blinker was saying, he didn't go off to the right. He took the highway to Morlaix. I took off after him.

Since we'd planned to take that detour in any case, Barbie wasn't noticing anything, or, if she was, she was being careful not to let me know it. On any open road in almost no time at all, Baby's speed would have overtaken the two guys in that car, but that's a heavily traveled stretch of highway and it was the wrong time of day. St. Brieuc is a factory town and they've built a big industrial park at the edge of it. It was late afternoon, the end of the workday when every Frenchman and his brother is heading home to the *bonne femme* and the *bonne soupe*, and the roads choke up with traffic.

Those lugs up ahead were doing a lot of weaving in and

out from lane to lane. Baby, the way she handles, is great at that game, but there's not too much that even Baby can do about French drivers. A Frenchman is sweating it out in heavy traffic and suddenly a maniac comes zipping past his nose to slide in ahead of him. That's all it takes. Nobody has to give him any "*Allons, enfants de la patrie.*" That *enfant de la patrie* goes charging forward to close even the smallest gap, and from that time on he tailgates all the way. He isn't going to give any other lunatic as much as an inch. Nobody does that to him a second time.

We did our best, Baby and I, but all our best was giving us was to keep that car with the two lugs in it always in sight, but always held away from us by the tantalizing obstacle of a couple of intervening cars. It was a crawling pursuit, but it was all I could do to hold my place in that sluggish parade. I wasn't doing well. By the very nature of things, I was losing ground all the way. That car up ahead wasn't finding many openings, but it found an occasional one. I was finding none because, as the inevitable result of its maneuverings, it was leaving in its wake a solid phalanx of tailgaters.

Somewhere along there Barbie began plucking at my elbow. I shook her off. She grabbed at my arm. I pushed her off me and told her to sit still and behave herself. If she couldn't do that, she could climb over into the back seat and join Mathilda. Maybe she could learn some automobile manners from the pup. She wasn't listening. I blew.

"That's enough," I said. "Get back there with the other bitch and leave me alone."

She let go of my arm. Retreating to the far side of the seat, she sulked. After a couple of minutes she started talking.

"You promised," she said.

"What did I promise?"

"Guimiliau. We were going down to Guimiliau."

"We'll get there."

"No, we won't. That was the turnoff back there. I saw the sign. You went right by it."

"Did I? That's all right. It'll still be there tomorrow. She's been there in the mouth of hell for hundreds of years. She'll be there awhile longer. She's not going any place."

"And *we* aren't either," Barbie said. "We could have been out of this traffic."

"You didn't see them?" I asked.

She said nothing.

I took my eyes off the traffic for a moment to grab a look at her. She had her lower lip caught between her teeth and she looked awful. The kid looked scared.

"Then, you did see them and you hoped I hadn't," I said.

"No," she said. "Who?"

"Who do you think? The two guys."

"Them? Here? Are you sure?"

"I'm sure. They're right there, four cars ahead, and they're trying to shake us off. I'm not about to be shaken off."

"Why, Matt? Let them go. What do you want to go messing with them for?"

"What for?" I said. "They're here and they're trying to shake me, because they want to wait till they can take me on their terms in their own good time. They can't do anything here. They can't do anything now. They can't because they don't operate in any crowd of witnesses. But here and now are okay for me. I can operate before witnesses. That's why."

"I'd rather you didn't," she said.

"That's got to mean that you'd rather I waited till they

got around to blowing my head off," I told her. "Sorry, lady. I like my head, so this has to be one time I can't indulge you."

"Just yesterday you weren't afraid of them," she said.

"And today I'm not afraid of them. They're the ones who are running. I'm not. They bother me and it's time I did something about it."

"The police?" she asked.

"You can go to the head of the class."

"Even though you know how I feel?"

"I'm sorry about the way you feel, but I think you're crazy. At least I hope you're crazy."

"What does that mean?" she asked.

"Think about it," I said. "It'll come to you."

"You think that I . . . ?" she began.

"I've been trying *not* to think it. It's getting harder all the time."

"You're a bastard," she said.

"That's me, like William, and I'm on my way to being a conqueror."

While we had been batting it back and forth that way, those guys up ahead had found another gap and were now five cars ahead and there was no way I could close it. I was handling it as best I could. My best was no way good enough. Exasperation and frustration had been building up inside me. They were poisoning me. Barbie had picked a bad time for bugging me. I had to take my frustration out on somebody, and she was there and you can't say she wasn't asking for it.

My best hope lay with nothing I myself could do. I could only hold my place and pray that they weren't going to find too many more openings for their weaving in and out. It wasn't going to take too many more before I would be so far away from them that, come a spot where the traffic thinned out, they could be off and gone before I could know which turnoff they had taken for their escape route.

Then it came and, even before I knew what it was going to be, I was cursing it. One great big son-of-a-gun of a truck came out of a side road to nose into our stream of traffic, and the car just ahead of me was letting him in. That was going to fix me. That big job, filled full and overflowing with cabbages, was going to be sitting there ahead of me and all view of the road beyond would be cut off. There was nothing for me to do but sit there in that stream of crawling traffic and count heads—cabbage heads.

It was no good watching the road ahead any more. I had seen cabbages—maybe never in such great numbers before, but who counts? I turned to look at Barbie. She was grinning from ear to ear. In her happiest times with me—and we'd had happy times—she'd never shown anything to touch this look of pure joy. As soon as she realized that I was looking at her, she had the good grace to wipe it away, but I had seen it. I preferred the cabbages.

I turned back to them and only just in time. The damnedest thing was happening. The truck tailgate fell open. It was a dump truck. The truckbed tilted up and it dumped. Cabbages came cascading out, a mountain of cabbages. The rolling heads bounced off cars and heaped up to fill the road. Up ahead the emptied truckbed settled back to the horizontal and the truck went chugging on, leaving the road behind it blocked with a barricade of cabbages.

Baby was equal to the emergency. As I've told you often enough, she handles. At the slow pace we'd been going in that choked-up traffic, bringing her to a stop in next to no space was easy. The cars behind us didn't do as well.

The guy behind me banged into Baby's tail, and car after car as far back as I could see piled into the mess. It was one of those chain-reaction smashups. It couldn't have been otherwise.

Everything came to a stop, but only on our side of the cabbage barrier. The traffic up ahead, with that damn truck trundling in its wake, was moving along. Somewhere in the middle of it those two guys were making their getaway. There was no helping that. I just had to take it.

I climbed out to see how much damage Baby had taken on her tail. It wasn't easy. The road was covered with cabbages. It was wall-to-wall kraut. It wasn't possible to get a foot down between the heads, and as soon as you put even a little weight on them, the heads rolled under you. It was like trying to walk on a field of gigantic ball bearings. By hanging on to Baby all the way, I managed to work my way around in back of her. Other guys out of other cars were trying to do the same thing. Some were getting it made, and some went sprawling among the rolling heads.

Baby was damaged, but her hurt looked to be little more than cosmetic. She had some scratches and dents, and one of her taillights had been smashed, but there was nothing that would stop her rolling, if she was ever going to get any rolling room.

When I came back out from behind her, I saw something new. Nobody was going to clear the cabbage mountain away to open up the highway. That side road out of which the crazy truck had come was now blocked edge to edge with cars and pickup trucks. They were just standing there empty. Their drivers had poured out onto the highway and had taken position to stand guard over the cabbage mountain.

They were big guys, ham-handed and heavy-shouldered. Their faces were leathery. They had known years of sun and rain and wind. They looked tough and they looked determined and they had come prepared. Some of them were carrying shotguns and some had hunting rifles. They looked dangerous but not nearly as dangerous as the bucks who had come with axe handles and pitchforks.

I'd worked my way forward with those damn cabbage heads rolling under my feet, and I was hanging on alongside Barbie. She was just sitting there and staring.

"Matt," she said, "what is it? What's with them? Are they crazy, or what?"

I had the answer for her. I was remembering the item I had seen in *Figaro*.

"They're farmers," I said, "and they're French. They're pulling a farmers' strike. They don't like what the Common Market does to the price of cabbages, so they go to the barricades. In Paris it would have been cobblestones. Here it's cabbages."

"But what can they accomplish?"

"This," I said. "They can tie up rush-hour traffic. They can raise hell. This is France, Baby."

"This is awful," she said.

"What's awful? It's a break for your friends. They got away."

"You don't think they're my friends, Matt. You can't think that."

"What else can I think?"

"What I've been telling you."

"When you saw that they were going to get away, you couldn't have been happier."

"Of course I was happy. I hate fights, and you were dead set on getting into one. I was happy because now you couldn't."

"And the next time they take a shot at me?" I asked.

"I know," she mumbled. "I know. I'm all mixed up. I'm not making much sense, Matt. I know it. A lot of the time I don't. Part of it is the way I am about having my own way. I hate myself for it, but it's the way I am. I wanted to go down and see that calvary, and you weren't going to take me. I was all worked up because I wasn't having my own way, and then this happened and you weren't having yours either. I know I shouldn't have felt that way, but it was a moment of triumph—nasty triumph. That's the way I am, Matt. I don't understand how you can like me at all."

"I'm not sure I do like you, doll," I said. "Your body's all right. I have no trouble liking that, but I wish I could know what you have inside your head."

"I keep telling you. I wish you believed me."

The other drivers were out of their cars and working at clearing the road. Words were flying back and forth between them and the farmers who were guarding the barrier. If I'd given it my full attention, I could have learned a lot of new French words. I'd always admired the extensive vocabulary of Paris cabbies, but compared to the aroused Breton citizenry and the embattled Breton farmers, those cabbies are tongue-tied. Their best efforts rate as little more than Sunday-school stuff.

The farmers were doing nothing to interfere with the road clearing. It was all right with them as long as nothing was done to diminish their cabbage mountain. So long as we were gathering up the heads that were rolling loose on the road and adding them to the heap over which they were standing guard, they offered no objection. They didn't want to keep us stranded there all night. It was all right with them if we got things cleared so that we could back away from their barricade and find some other way of going where we'd been headed.

Those farmers, after all, were Frenchmen. They were out to create as much confusion and paralysis as they could manage, but they wouldn't go so far as to keep any man from his dinner. There are some things that must always take precedence over politics, and even over economics.

No few of the stranded drivers were making the best of their discomfiture. As they gathered the heads up off the road, they didn't heap them on the barricade pile. They tossed them into their cars. Food is food.

I joined the workers, and Barbie came out of the car and fell to as well. Mathilda tried to join us, but we dissuaded her. Meanwhile the road behind us was slowly clearing. One by one the cars were backing away and managing a U-turn to take off back the way they had come. After a while the cars directly behind us pulled out, and Baby had maneuvering room.

Headed back toward St. Brieuc, our most direct way up to Perros-Guirec now would have been to take the Guingamp turnoff. I thought about it as I drove. This cabbage dumping was obviously an organized deal. Closing off just one highway would be a gesture. It would cause some confusion but little paralysis. A well-organized farmers' strike would shut off all the highways in the area.

The back roads, however, the farm roads, would remain open. The striking farmers would need those for their own mobility. That highway up through Guingamp would get us nowhere. We were going to need a zigzag of little country roads to take us to Perros-Guirec. I asked myself if I wanted to go to Perros-Guirec, having a good idea of what I would find waiting for me there. As soon as the question had popped into my head, however, I was answering myself and the answer was an emphatic yes. Twice they had come on me when I wasn't expecting anything. This third time was going to be different. I was going up there and I was going to make it different.

We were riding along in another traffic jam. All those cars that had been turned around by the rolling heads of cabbage were swarming back along the highway, and fresh battalions of homegoing cars were meeting us and, getting the word, were doing U-turns and adding to our jam.

I spotted a side road and the signpost said GUIMILIAU. I edged to the outer lane and took it. Barbie slid over and cuddled against my arm.

"You're sweet," she said.

"I'm pulling out of this traffic," I told her.

"And going to Guimiliau," she said.

"Why not?" I said. "Since we can't use the highway, Guimiliau is on our way."

"On the way to where?"

"Perros-Guirec, the beach. That's where you wanted to go, isn't it?"

"If you think they'll be there, we can go someplace else."

"No, we can't," I said. "They'll be there, and this time I'll be ready for them. I want those goons."

"Going on west," she said, "the map shows all kinds of beaches along the coast."

"So close to Perros-Guirec that it makes no difference," I said. "Further along on this north coast you no longer have sand beaches. They're gravel. Down the west coast, of course, there's Quiberon. That's good sand down there."

She shook her head.

"I don't want to go there. I won't like it there."

"Don't get so intense about it, kid," I said. "I've already told you. It's going to be Perros-Guirec."

V.

We were on a winding country road, but we weren't out of traffic. Other drivers had had the same idea. The road looped away from the highway, passed through some small villages, and then, just a few kilometers short of St. Brieuc, rejoined the highway. Other drivers had looked at the map, and the locals would know the roads in any case. Going this way added only a mile or two, but it was taking us past the stretch of highway that was most choked up.

We came into Guimiliau, and that calvary she had been dead set on seeing was the biggest thing in sight. Nobody could miss it. It stood in the parish close just off the road. I pulled Baby off to the side and found a place I could park her. We walked in to look at the calvary. We were alone with it. All the other cars were going straight on through. They had no interest in the mouth of hell. They were headed for dinner.

That calvary was something to see. When a thing is bad enough, it takes on some kind of distinction. It was big, and every inch of it was hysterics in granite. It had taken a lot of doing to carve that hardest of stones into this mass of jumbled confusion. The crucifixion part of it wasn't too hard to make out. The cross was the only thing on it that wasn't tied into knots and writhing. All the rest of it was so mixed up and in such violent motion that it would make the Laocoön look like a serene work of art. Bible stories and local Breton myths were there, all jammed up together. It took a lot of study to separate one from the other.

The guidebook had a picture of the Catell-Gollet in the mouth-of-hell detail. With the help of the picture, we searched it out. She was there all right, and with her a devil who had a big pair of forceps. He was dragging her down by a tooth. If any girl too much given to flirting ever took the trouble to go to Guimiliau and find the unfortunate Catherine, it seemed to me she would be likely to come away with a warning not to avoid flirting but to stay clear of dentists.

Barbie was delighted with her. I couldn't see why, but *chacun à son goût* and *de gustibus non est disputandum*, and there's no accounting for tastes. She wanted a picture of the fool thing. Across the road from the parish close there was a little shop that sold postcards.

"They'll have some of her," Barbie said. "They're bound to. Be a darling and go see. If they have more than one view, get them all."

"How about you coming along and picking them out for yourself?" I suggested.

"I'm going to take some snaps of it," she said. "The postcards are just in case my pictures don't come out. It's so late already that the light isn't too good, and it'll be getting worse by the minute."

She was on her way over to Baby to get her camera. There wasn't a chance that she would get any kind of a picture. Even in good light the dull gray of that granite wouldn't photograph well. It doesn't give you any sharply marked shadows. In the light she had, with dusk setting in, she was going to get nothing more than a picture of a gray scrambled egg. I said nothing. If Barbie wanted to snap pictures, she would snap pictures. I had learned that much about this girl early on. She had a whim of iron.

I went into the little shop to buy her the postcards. They had a big disorderly rack of the things, with nothing sorted out. The assortment covered the whole of Brittany—views of the coast, views of sea-washed pink rocks, pictures of lobsters, pictures of mounds of oyster shells, pictures of fishing boats and fishermen, pictures of the Dinard Casino, pictures of the babes in those tall, starched caps. You name it. They had it. I had to search through the lot for pictures of the calvary, and then sort through those for the kid in the mouth of hell. They had them, a couple of middle-distance shots and three close-ups taken from different angles. I collected the lot. There was nobody in the little shop, but there was a bell on the counter. I tapped it and slowly an old woman came creaking out of a back room.

She took the cards from me and counted them. Then she took my money. Then she counted the cards again and brought out a piece of brown paper bag and a stub of pencil. Laboriously she did the arithmetic. I guess she didn't know how to multiply. It was five cards at twenty *centimes* each. She wrote down the twenty centimes and then wrote it down four more times, building a column of the five identical numbers. Before she tried to add them up, she ticked them off with her pencil, counting to make certain she had five. Then she counted the cards again. That did it. She was finally ready to do the sum. Having added it and come to one *franc*, she went back and checked her addition. It was only after that that she was ready to take the franc out of my hand and let me have the cards. Even then I couldn't have them until she'd put them in a bag for me. That meant hunting under her little counter to find a bag.

I came out of the shop and headed for the calvary. On the way into the parish close I passed Baby where I had parked her. Mathilda had been sprawled across the back seat dozing. Now she wasn't there. I thought nothing much of it. It seemed to be the sensible thing for Barbie, when she went to the car for her camera, to have let Mathilda out for a run. I came around from the far side of the calvary expecting that Barbie would be there, doing her futile photography. She was nowhere in sight, and neither was Mathilda.

It didn't worry me. There had been more than enough time for picture-taking while I had been tied up with the old woman in the little shop. Now Barbie would be off in the fields somewhere letting Mathilda have a good run. I just leaned against the calvary and waited for them to come back.

They didn't come back. The wave of traffic had trickled away to nothing. The little old woman put up the shutters on her one small shop window and locked the shop door. I was alone with that mass of writhing granite. I looked at my watch. They had been gone a long time, time enough for her to have taken Mathilda off on a dozen runs. If I hadn't been certain that those two men were blocked away from this stretch of country by a mountain of cabbages, I would have been quicker to begin worrying.

If one thing was certain, it was that those guys were out of the picture. The cabbages lay between them and any but the most circuitous access to this back road. They could, of course, by doing a wide circle over a web of other back roads, come around onto this one; but, even if done at top speed, it would have been a time-consuming journey and there had been nothing like that much time.

Waiting, I'd been smoking cigarette after cigarette. I reached into my pocket for another and found that I'd run out. I moved over to Baby for a fresh pack, and that is when I saw it. It lay on the front seat, a neatly folded piece of letter paper. I picked it up and unfolded it.

It read:

"Dearest Matt: You're going to hate me and, of course, you should. I would have liked it if you didn't hate me, but I have to do it this way because it has to be that you should hate me. Any other way, you'd be coming after me, and you mustn't do that. I've gone back to Johnny. That's why we had to come here today. It had all been arranged. I was meeting him here. I was mad at him and I used you to make him jealous. I didn't expect that you'd be sweet and I'd get to hate myself for using you. But Johnny's my man, and you must see that he showed me how much I mean to him. I didn't like his way of doing it. He could have gotten you killed, but, after all, it was for me. It was because he wanted me back and he wanted it that much. Try to understand how important it is to be wanted that much, but don't forgive me, Matt. I'm no good, and I'm with the man who deserves me. You're a wonderful guy, Matt. You deserve better. So don't come after me. Go find her, Matt, and be happy."

It was signed "Barbie."

The note was clear enough, but it said even more than the words she had written. The paper was hotel stationery from the place in Vernon where we'd been the previous night. The ink was purple. The hotel ink had been purple. I'd noticed that on the bill they'd given me. I also knew the ballpoint Barbie carried. Its ink was black, not purple.

If there was anything that the actual wording of the note had left unclear, the evidence of the letter paper and the color of the ink filled the gap. I'd been used and, when she had finished using me, she had made her arrangements. Sucking me into taking Mathilda for that morning run, she'd had the time alone to telephone her precious Johnny and tell him that she was ready to come back to him. They had arranged to meet at Guimiliau. That explained her desperate need for coming to the mouth of hell and coming there on that day and none other.

They had arranged it, and right down to the last moment she had played me. I was asking myself why she had needed that. Certainly she could have told me she was going back to him. What could I have done about it other than let her go? If she had wanted it that way, I would even have taken her back to him. Why did her game have to be carried all the way? Was it necessary that she should leave me with this feeling that I had been suckered, that nothing of what we'd had together had ever been real? She was calling herself no good, and that evidently she was, but there are degrees. She had carried hers to the ultimate degree.

I had been dead set on going to Perros-Guirec, promising myself a shot at meeting the two goons on more even terms. This, of course, changed everything, but not enough. I still wanted those two. In my heart I wanted Johnny too, but I was working at talking myself out of that. Neither of them was going to think, even for a minute, that I cared enough to go and fight him for her. The two I was going to hunt out in Perros-Guirec would be enough. Barbie and her Johnny would get the word.

I climbed aboard Baby and pulled out. It was a tree-shaded road, narrow and winding. Although in northern European midsummers between sunset and the coming of dark you have a long interval of twilight, clouds had been rolling in and a heavy fog had settled on the road. Between the fog and the clouds and the tree cover, visibility for the road's twists and turns was heading down toward zero.

I was aching to ram the accelerator down to the floor. I was a raging maniac, and I had the feeling that driving like one would make me feel better. On that road and in those conditions it was impossible. Why I should have had the sense to recognize that, I don't know. I drove carefully, holding the speed down and staring hard at the road ahead.

I had gone only a little more than a kilometer when I heard it. It was a dog. It howled, and after an interval of whimpering it howled again. Can you know a dog's voice? I thought I did. The howl could have been any dog's howl. I didn't know. I'd never heard Mathilda howl, but I thought I knew the whimper.

I told myself to ignore it. It was my imagination. It had to be some other dog. He'd picked them up and they'd taken off. It was too crazy to think that they would then have hung about the neighborhood. They'd had a good hunk of lead time. By now they'd be up and away, burning up the road back to Dinard.

I came around a bend and my lights picked her up. I was almost on top of her. I was still telling myself it was just a dog. It couldn't be Mathilda. Seen through the fog, she was just a moving shape low to the road. But for hearing the whimpering, I mightn't have known whether it was a dog or some other animal. I pulled to a stop, still telling myself it wasn't Mathilda and even playing with the thought that Mathilda might never have been her name. I was wondering whether the thing could have started that far back. Had she yelled my name that morning on the beach as a way of inducing a pickup, renaming her dog on the spot so she could pull it off?

I came out of the car and the dog jumped at me. It was Mathilda, and she was carrying on just as she had that night on the Mont St. Michel battlements. She was running at me. She was whimpering. She was running from me into the bushes at the side of the road, then looking back at me again when I didn't follow. I had a flashlight in the glove compartment. I took it out and followed Mathilda into the undergrowth.

It wasn't far to go. The stuff was thick and tangled at the roadside, but someone had been through there not too long before. There was an opening of sorts where the growth was torn and trampled. To the eye it wasn't there, but, shoving my way through it, I found less resistance than I would have expected.

I don't know what I thought I was going to find. The one idea that popped at me was too screwy to hold. Was I going to find them in there making love under the trees? So hungry for each other that they couldn't wait? With the fog dripping from leaves and twigs, it was wet in there. The ground squished under my shoes. Could anyone have been hungry enough to be lying in that?

The dog was ahead of me all the way. Once we'd gone into the brush I could only hear her, I couldn't see her. She slithered through the shrubbery and it closed in immediately behind her. It didn't matter. I had two things to guide me, the sound of her whimpering and that trail that had been broken by someone passing through before me.

Abruptly the whimpering stopped, followed by the long-drawn-out ululation of a howl. I broke through the last of the tangle, and my light picked up a small area where under a clump of pine trees the carpeting of needles had kept the forest floor clear of undergrowth. Mathilda was sitting there. She was up on her haunches with her muzzle raised, funneling her howl toward the treetops. Barbie lay beside her. The light fell on her face and throat, and I knew. She was dead. The bruises on her throat read all too clearly. Hands had closed around it. The thumbs had pressed in. She had been strangled.

Knowing that it was hopeless made no difference. I

dropped down beside her and tried everything. It was no good. There was no flicker of life left in her. For the first moments there I could think of nothing I wanted but to squat down alongside Mathilda and match the dog howl for howl. I was making no sense. Every idea I had was flipping over and turning inside out. I couldn't think. I could find no way to understand it.

How long I just stayed there, biting down my rage and horror and trying to find some way of coming to terms with this thing I couldn't grasp, I don't know. I tore myself away from thinking any of that and made a stab at concentrating on what I had to.

My first idea was to load the body into the car and take it to the nearest police station, wherever that was. Thinking about that, I told myself it would be wrong. The police would want her left exactly as I'd found her. I was going to have to go for the police and bring them back here with me, but that meant leaving her there alone with no one to watch over her.

Sickening pictures crowded into my mind, animals coming into the clearing and feeding on the body. I had to fight those pictures off. I was going to force myself to leave her. I took my jacket off and used it to cover her. I put it over her face and over as much of the rest of her as I could manage by pulling to full stretch.

Calling Mathilda, I started back to the car. Mathilda followed me a few whimpering steps, but then she returned to the body. I called to her again, but this time she wouldn't come. She just squatted beside Barbie and howled. I went back and picked her up in my arms. Crashing back through to the road was a lot harder than it had been coming in, now that I was doing it with an armload of desperately squirming basset.

I made it out to the car and, looking back, saw where the

undergrowth had closed in behind me. I flashed my light around, trying to pick up some landmark. I was going to have to be sure of finding this spot again when I returned with the police. I saw nothing I could use as a marker. I stripped my tie off. That left me with only one hand for holding Mathilda. She squirmed free and shot back into the undergrowth before I could make a grab at her. Within moments I was hearing her back in there. She was howling alongside the body.

I tied the tie to one of the bushes that overhung the road. Then I went back in after Mathilda. Now it was different. Now she was wary of me. For what seemed like forever, the two of us were in there circling the body while I tried to catch her. Sickeningly, it was taking me back to the Grande Plage at Dinard where all this had started, and it had taken the two of us to catch her. Here, however, her range was more limited. She wasn't taking off into the woods or diving into the thickets where she could slither through and I would be held up by the tangle. She was staying close to the body. Eventually I managed to catch her.

This time I carried her back to the car and tried to settle her on the seat beside me. As soon as I took my hand away to start the car, however, she was up and out and disappearing again into the bush. It was no good. I had to leave her, and as I drove away, I was wondering why I had been so dead set on taking the dog with me. Maybe the pup knew better than I did. I wasn't leaving the body alone.

I had been thinking that I would go back to Guimiliau. I'd seen the place and I knew that it was too small to have anything like a policeman. As villages go, it was as near to nothing as a village can be, just a few houses, that little shop, and the crazy parish close. I doubted that I'd even find a telephone there.

I remembered the road map. Going on the way I'd been going, I'd be hitting another town. It was not much further than the road back to Guimiliau, possibly a kilometer more at the most. I had gone the better part of halfway to it. I didn't expect that it was going to be a big place, but it rated a slightly larger dot on the map. It looked a better bet than Guimiliau.

That modicum of good sense I'd had and that had served to hold my speed down within sane limits had now left me. I took that winding, fog-shrouded road at a clip that was suicidal. I came out on a stretch that ran straight and on higher ground. There the road lifted out of the fog and I put Baby to it. We came roaring into that bigger dot on the map at a murderous clip.

It was a one-street town, but on that one street there was a small café and some men sitting at tables out in front of it. I yelled for the *gendarmerie*. The guys at the tables just stared at me. I was a strange sight. They were going to look me over and take me in before they would engage in any conversation.

Inside the place there was a beefy buck behind the bar. He roared back at me.

To get at what he was saying I had to dig through a thick Breton accent. That fully developed Breton sound is to French about what a County Cork brogue is to English. I may not have gotten it in its full rich detail, but the general meaning came through. I was a guy who didn't have to go looking for the *gendarmes*. The way I drove, they would come looking for me.

I vaulted out of Baby and ran into the place yammering for a telephone. There was no telephone.

Where was the nearest telephone?

"*Les pompiers.*"

He pointed up the street and I spotted it, a shiny

firehouse. It was the only thing in sight that looked anything less than a couple of hundred years old. In that town it looked like the year after next. From where I was, I could see that it was locked up tight. I could see no way to get in there short of setting off a fire alarm.

"On the road from Guimiliau . . ." I began.

The word "Guimiliau" touched them off. The guys came crowding in from the tables outside and formed a chrous to back up the barman.

For Guimiliau I was going the wrong way. Guimiliau was back the way I had come. I must have passed right through it without knowing I was there.

I had to fight my way through their explanations to get my first word in. A couple of them were grabbing me by the elbows and trying to point me in the right direction. I shook them off and started screaming.

"*Non, non, non.*"

That got them back to where they'd started. They clumped around me and stared. I was even more peculiar and interesting than they had first thought.

"A young woman," I explained, "she is dead. She has been murdered. She is back there on the Guimiliau road. I must find the police. I must bring them to her."

The big guy popped through a door behind the bar. One of the others slid around behind the *zinc* and took over on the bottles and the glassware. Around me a wild argument swirled. I tried to grab at the meaning. It had to be that what I'd told them was under discussion, but that Breton speech is tough enough for a foreign ear under any circumstances. Roared at full throttle and with everybody yelling at once, it's just about hopeless.

At first I thought they were ignoring what I'd told them. They didn't seem to be talking about murder at all. They were talking cabbages. Gradually, though, I began to catch the drift of it. It was the farmers' strike. I was in the middle of a controversy between a pro-strike faction and an anti-strike faction. The anti-strikers were denouncing violence. They'd known all along that no good could come of such wild and sinfully wasteful antics as dumping cabbages out on the roads. Violence, they were saying, leads to more violence, and now the inevitable had happened. A woman was dead.

The pro-strike faction was countering with the drop in the farmers' cabbage price. They were fighting to keep the bread in the mouths of their wives and children. If anyone wanted to talk about murder, that was murder, reducing children to a state of starvation. Also, a murdered woman on the Guimiliau road had nothing to do with the strike. Nobody had dumped any cabbages on that little back road. The farmers had better sense than that. Nobody wasted cabbages on Guimiliau.

I couldn't say that I hadn't started something, but it appeared to be nothing that could have been any good to anyone. I still had to get through to the gendarmes, and I wanted to do it quickly. I had to get back to Barbie. I thought wildly of setting off a fire alarm, but I didn't have even the first idea of how that could be done short of some small act of arson, like setting fire to the little zinc bar.

I tried to shout them down and remind them that the gendarmes were needed, but they took time out from their argument only to give me what I assume was intended as a lot of reassuring little pats. While the lot of them were getting red in the face roaring at each other, they were treating me as though I was the excitable type who needed calming down.

I was about to haul out of there to jump into Baby and head for what looked like an even larger dot on the map, when the barman came running from the direction of the firehouse. Evidently he was one of the pompiers. He was wearing his shiny fire helmet. Reaching in the door of the café, he grabbed me by the arm and hauled me outside.

"I will go with you to the dead woman," he said.

"The gendarmes," I insisted.

"They will come. I have telephoned them. They will meet us on the road."

I whacked him on the back and told him he was a good man.

He whacked me on the back and told me that I was a wonderful, crazy driver. With that, he vaulted the door and settled himself in Baby. I'd never seen a mass of beef that light on its feet.

I jumped in beside him. He held on to his fire helmet with both hands and grinned at me. He was set for a wonderful and crazy ride. I couldn't dissappoint him and I didn't want to. It wasn't until we were off that high straight stretch and back in the hollow with the fog around us that I slacked off the speed. I thought I could count on Mathilda's howling to mark the spot for me, but I wasn't certain of it. Would she keep it up indefinitely, or would she run out of voice? I had to take it slowly if I was to spot the tie I'd left hanging from the bush.

I didn't need it. A good stretch before we reached the spot we heard Mathilda. She was still in full cry, a session of howling and a session of those whimpering runs out to the road and back. I pulled up and my pompier spotted the tie.

"You said a woman?" he asked.

"Yes, a woman, strangled to death."

"With the cravat?"

I explained about the tie and took him through the underbrush to the body and Mathilda howling beside it. He lifted my jacket and looked at her face.

"She was beautiful," he said.

"Yes, she was."

"A beautiful face and a beautiful body. Of course, she was raped."

"No," I said. "She wasn't raped."

"You have looked?"

"I haven't looked. It isn't necessary."

"But it is most necessary," he said, reaching for the waistband of her slacks.

I pushed his hands away. Mathilda started for him, baring her teeth. He gave up on it. Whether it was out of respect for Mathilda or for me I don't know.

"It is not necessary," I repeated. "I knew her and I know who she was with. He was her lover. He wouldn't have needed to rape her."

"You knew her?"

"Yes."

"And you know her lover?"

"I've seen him."

"And you let him get away."

"I wasn't here."

"Where were you?"

"Back in Guimiliau."

I was trying to think. This question-and-answer routine was getting in the way of it. I suggested to my pompier friend that it might be a good idea if he was out on the road to flag down the police when they came. He could lead them to the body.

"They'll know the place," he said. "They'll see your car. I told them a Porsche."

"They might not find their way in here," I persisted.

"Yes," he agreed. "They are gendarmes. It surprises one that they can even find their way into their pants."

With that he went back out to the road. I was left alone

with Barbie and Mathilda. The dog had given up on the howling. She was staying close to me, rubbing against my ankles. I stroked her and I squatted down to scratch her under the chin. She always liked that. She responded with a half-hearted tail wag. Obviously she wasn't feeling up to anything like her usual exuberance.

Up to that point I had been trying to cope with wildly divergent, contradictory thoughts. With my hand under the dog's muzzle, something came to me that began to give my thinking some direction. Mathilda's muzzle was dry. My hand was not coming away from it sticky. I turned the flashlight on her and examined her.

I was remembering her as she had been when she came back from her pursuit of that fugitive goon on the Mont St. Michel causeway. There had been blood on her muzzle then. Now, on even the closest examination, I was finding none. I knelt on the pine needles beside her and felt her all over, her legs, along her ribs, her haunches, her head.

I was exploring for injuries, for some tender spot that might bring from her even a small yelp of pain. I found none. It was something to think about. The attack on Barbie that night on the Mont St. Michel battlements had turned the dog savage. She had been in there and fighting, sinking her teeth into the lug. Now she was showing no evidence of having put up any sort of fight. Nobody'd had any need for fighting her off. She hadn't been manhandled. She hadn't been kicked.

I was having a picture of the pup standing by with her tail wagging while the hands had gone around Barbie's throat and all life had been squeezed out of the girl. There had to be a reason for such passivity. It was incredibly out of character for Mathilda. I thought about it, and it came to me that it both was and wasn't out of character.

Time and again the dog had seen me with my hands on

her mistress, and she had always taken it with languor or with tail-wagging canine approval. I couldn't believe that it could be explained by assuming that Mathilda, between her long, silky ears, harbored an intelligence that could make distinctions between affectionate and hostile intent.

It had to be that she made distinctions between acts of a man she had learned to accept and the acts of a stranger. The conclusion was inevitable. I could read the evidence only one way. This time it had been Barbie's Johnny himself. He hadn't sent any hired goons to act for him. It had been a man Mathilda knew and trusted. The dog had seen them make love. She'd had no way of knowing that this time it was to be something different.

Mathilda had had no way of knowing, and Barbie'd had no way of knowing. I could see her going into these woods with him happily enough and, until it was too late, never knowing what he had in his mind to do to her.

She couldn't possibly have known. Those men had grabbed her back at Mont St. Michel, but they had taken pains not to hurt her. They had merely been kidnaping her to take her back to her Johnny. Then the second time, at Les Andelys, they had aimed their shooting only at me. I was seeing her as she had stood there on the battlements exposing herself to their fire and drawing not even the first shot.

She had done that in full confidence that she would not be their target. With that same confidence she had gone into the woods with Johnny. That also was something that needed thinking about. What had brought about the change? Obviously he had given his orders, and they had been that she was not to be hurt. Was it that he had been meaning to kill her all along, but he had wanted her saved for him? Had it been something he wanted to do himself?

It was conceivable, but another thought came at me to

contradict it. He'd been wanting her back and he'd been prepared to go to all lengths to bring her back, even if it involved knocking me off. It seemed to me that it had only been the morning of this last day that she'd made this arrangement for going back to him. It had to be that the meeting at Guimiliau had been set up, while I had been out with Mathilda for the dog's morning run.

Earlier at Mont St. Michel, when the two goons had made their attempt at taking her, she had been savage in her determination to thwart them. She hadn't wanted to be taken back to him then. But now, these few days later, she had changed her mind. I tried to fight away from the thought of what had brought about the change.

I couldn't rid myself of it. I had to recognize that it made too much sense. The rifle fire at Les Andelys had been for real, Johnny's boys had been out to kill me. She had seen it. She had been convinced of it. It was that attempt that had changed her.

It explained everything. It explained the wording of the note she had left me. It explained the way she had gone about pulling out. She had made it as sneaky as it possibly could be, and she had set it up to be as wounding as possible. I could call it sadism, but I couldn't make myself believe that. It made better sense and it seemed more like her that she should have used those methods in an effort to turn me off. I was to be angered and disgusted. I was to want no more of her. I was to be cut away from any wish to go after her to try to win her back. All of this she had considered necessary because she had been afraid for me.

Could it also explain the change in him? Fearful for me, she called him to tell him that she was leaving me and going back to him, but she had not really changed. When she told me that she was through with him, she had been telling the truth.

Then, what had happened in the short time after she'd made the switch at Guimiliau? I could imagine two possibilities. She had told him straight out that she was through with him, and, even though she had also told him that she was likewise through with me, that hadn't appeased him. The other possibility was that she had been unable to sustain her act with him. He had realized that she was only pretending and that he wasn't to have her back after all.

I didn't want to believe that she had died on my account. The thought, however, was there. I couldn't shake it off.

VI.

I had expected that the gendarmes would give me a hard time, and of course they did. I had known all along that my story would take a great deal of believing, but hearing the words as they came out of me, I couldn't even make myself feel that they were believable. I fell back on telling myself that they would have to believe me. Not even an idiot would concoct a story that feeble. Thinking about what I was telling them, I did have the thought that I had one thing going for me: I had gone for the police. I had stood by waiting to tell them this absurd story of mine. I'd made no attempt to take off for parts unknown.

I told them the truth and nothing but the truth. I cannot say that I told them the whole truth. One significant detail I kept to myself. In describing the attempt the two men made at Les Andelys, I said they had been firing on us. I didn't tell them that, given the best opportunity, they had directed no fire at Barbie. Their effort there had been directed at me alone. That item, I thought, would contribute nothing. It would serve only to confuse them.

I had more than enough trouble explaining why the episode at Mont St. Michel had not been reported to the police, and even more difficulty explaining how, in talking to the gendarmes at the Château Gaillard the girl and I could have confused ourselves with rabbits. I tried to convince them that it had been a matter of delicacy on Barbie's part. She had been living with one man and had gone off with another. It is the sort of thing a woman likes to keep private.

Judging the situation from their policeman's view of the world, they were not persuaded that a woman, who lived with one man and at peril of her life abandoned him for another, would set any considerations of delicacy above concern for her safety. They searched me. They searched the car. They, of course, examined the body and the surrounding terrain. The fact that all these operations had to be carried on in the face of Mathilda's determined opposition pleased them not at all.

Under normal conditions the French are fools about dogs. If you've been in a restaurant in France where someone is accompanied by a dog, you'll know how it is. You'll have seen the kind of service the pooch gets. I remember one day in Paris when an American woman came in accompanied by a poodle. She ordered a drink for herself and asked for some water for the dog. The waiter wanted to know what kind of water. He suggested Perrier or, in the event that Fido might prefer still water, Evian.

"Just plain water," the woman said.

I've never forgotten the waiter's pained expression or the look of sympathy he cast in the direction of the animal whose mistress treated it with such lack of consideration. He did his best for the poodle. He served the water in a silver bowl.

Those, however, were normal conditions. Here at the outset, when they moved in on the body, Mathilda bared her teeth. I had to scoop her up and hold her before the flics could touch the body. When the time came for them to pat me down, I still had Mathilda in my arms and they couldn't come near me. I had to carry her out to the road and lock her in the police car, where of course she raised every kind of hell.

Their conclusion was that she was my dog and that she was up to no good. I gathered that in their minds it was an indication that I, too, was up to no good. I made the mistake of using her behavior to try to make a point. I explained to them that the fact that the man had been able to get his hands on Barbie's throat without any interference from Mathilda had to mean that the man had been someone Mathilda knew and trusted. They picked up on that.

"As she knows and trusts you," they said.

"And as she knew and trusted the other man," I was quick to add.

We were hours there in those woods. The road filled with police cars as wave after wave of gendarmes arrived. Eventually they brought in an ambulance and removed the body. Only then were they ready to take me and Mathilda in. Even that operation was not without its complications. Mathilda was raging. I had to pull her out of the police car and carry her to Baby. One of the gendarmes was assigned to ride with us, and there was some question of whether Mathilda would hold still for that, but I had her in the front seat beside me, and the flic rode in the back. Mathilda didn't take that in bad part. I think she was regarding him with aloof disdain.

My barman-pompier came along in one of the police cars. I had a battalion of them going before and behind me and, since they were all sounding their sirens, we zoomed along in an automotive bedlam. They took us to the gendarmerie in St. Brieuc, where I had to repeat my statement and it was taken down. I signed it.

I hadn't gone far with it before the whole atmosphere changed. There had been communications back and forth —Dinard, Mont St. Michel, Les Andelys, Paris. Inquiries made about Erridge established him as a solid citizen. There are advantages to being known in the right places. The fact that the solid citizen had been touring the provinces with a female of questionable character was now being taken with fine French aplomb.

"Unfortunate, Monsieur, but could it not happen to any of us?"

They came up with dossiers on Barbie and her Johnny. Something inside me curled up with resentment over the things they were telling me about Barbie. I expect it was fortunate that any of this Mathilda might have been taking in through those long, silken ears of hers was beyond her understanding. For my part, I had to put my resentment away and forget it. The record they read off to me was hard to take, but it fitted all too well with what I had known or had begun to guess.

John Gibbs and Barbara Maxwell—Interpol passed their names from country to country. There had been a bank holdup in Zurich and a jewel robbery in Milan, and these two had been in both places at the right time and had left both places immediately afterward. In neither place had the police been able to prove anything, but the word had been out. Wherever they turned up, they were to be watched.

The gendarmes knew that they had been in Dinard and had been frequenting the Casino, but by the time they'd had the word, it had been after the fact. They had both disappeared from Dinard. No report on Barbie and me had gone to Paris from Les Andelys. That business up at the Château Gaillard, after all, had been a nothing event. Some shots had been fired. The two of us had come up clean. Nobody had been hurt. Rabbit hunting out of season was against the law, but it had been too minor an infraction to be put into any report to Paris. It had been a file-and-forget item. Nobody among the Les Andelys police had picked up on the name Barbara Maxwell.

It was well after midnight before they turned Mathilda and me loose. We holed up for what was left of the night in a St. Brieuc hotel. In the morning I had the papers with my breakfast. They had two stories and they'd filled themselves up with them. One was the farmers' strike. They went to town with that one, pictures of the cabbage heads rolling about on the highways and shots of the embattled farmers mounted at their green barricade. The photographs had zoomed in on the pitchforks and the ax handles. Obviously those were better than any shotgun or rifles for giving the story the right agrarian look.

The other story was the murder of an American gun moll on the Guimiliau road. "Gun moll" was their term. French journalists pride themselves on their familiarity with the American *patois*. Even in Paris, though, they're likely to be out of date, and this was the provinces. They had no pictures of Barbie, but they had a beaut of Mathilda and me. They'd caught us when I was loading her into the police car.

They also had a picture of the car I'd stopped on the highway before the cabbage barricade made me lose it. The car had been found abandoned on the road just outside Perros-Guirec. The caption called it the murderer's car. That, of course, was something less than accurate. Maybe somebody had told the editor that a picture is worth a thousand words. He could have been thinking that even the wrong picture might be worth five hundred.

To me it was worth something, but I was trying to think what. Back there on the road those babies had been working hard at getting away from me. I could think of no reason why they would have been headed for Perros-Guirec unless it was because they'd been told it was where we were going.

They hadn't been following us. If they had been, I would have spotted them earlier in the day. Also, when I did spot them, they were riding along ahead of me—I was overtaking them. I could see no answer to that but that they had planned to be in Perros-Guirec before us with the idea of making yet another try at taking us in a setup where they would have the initiative. That they shouldn't have wanted an encounter on the highway made good sense. That wasn't the way they operated.

That they should have abandoned their car also made good sense. It could not have been anything but obvious to them that I knew the car and I knew the license number. I had given them a demonstration of that by the way I took off after them the moment I saw the car. From where I had been when I started chasing them, I could have picked up on them only through a recognition of car and registration number. I had been nowhere close enough and in nothing like the right angle for recognizing faces. It added up. They were going to be in Perros-Guirec waiting for us and they were going to try to take us by surprise. The car we could recognize had become a liability. They had needed a change of cars.

Am I saying that it added up? It did, but only to a point. Why would they be going to Perros-Guirec to lie in wait for us when their boss had set it up so that we would never be getting there? The first answer that came to me was that their communications had been that bad, but I couldn't make that one stick. The pair of lugs might fumble their assignment anytime. They had already done it twice, but John Gibbs was something else again. The bastard hadn't fumbled the job he had taken on to do himself. So why would he have sent them to Perros-Guirec?

I looked for some better reasons and I came up with two. One was that the man was a thorough type. He covered all bases. He'd had his plan for Guimiliau, but if, through some unforseen circumstance, that had gone awry, he'd had himself backstopped. In case he had failed at Guimiliau, they would be up in Perros-Guirec to take us on.

It seemed the most likely answer, but I worked at pushing it away so I could concentrate on the other. John Gibbs had taken for himself the joy of killing the woman who had walked out on him, but there was also the man who had taken her away from him. He'd sent his pair of goons on ahead to take care of that. Guimiliau had been for Barbie. Perros-Guirec had been set up for Matt Erridge.

I said the papers had no picture of Barbara Maxwell. They made up for it with pictures of Catell-Gollet, and they played the parallel for all it was worth. It was history repeating itself. The fallen woman had come to the mouth of hell and she had been dragged down in. They were crediting John Gibbs with some sort of ghoulish sense of the rightness of things. It made a good story, but I couldn't believe it. It just didn't seem to be his style. I did wonder why he had chosen Guimiliau, but try as I would, I was coming up with no answers to that.

I took Mathilda for a run. She wasn't at all herself. She was playing none of her usual games. The way she was acting, she might have been the obedience school's top graduate. Every step of the way she was at heel. She couldn't have stuck closer. She had lost Barbie; she was taking no chance on losing me.

I took the Guingamp road out of St. Brieuc, and I ran into another cabbage barricade. Like the other, it had been dumped the day before, but its defenders had made their point and had now abandoned it. The police were at work clearing the road. They were bulldozing the cabbages over onto the margins, but the road was not yet passable, and it looked as though it would be hours before it could be. Cabbage heads were rolling all over the place, and an army of thrifty Breton housewives was out on the road scooping them up for the soup pot. Since the gendarmes were not prepared to bulldoze the women over onto the road margins, the bulldozer progress was slowed down to a crawl.

They had a man out on the road to flag down traffic, and he was providing detour information. He sent me back to St. Brieuc to take the shore road and go up by way of St. Quay-Portrieux, Plouha, and Tréguier. It was the scenic route, but it wasn't Erridge's day for views of rocks and beach and sea. It wasn't my day for anything enjoyable. I was on a grim errand, and all I had on my mind was the fear that it would be a fruitless errand.

You can tell me she was no good and she got no more than was coming to her, but I'll never buy that. Nobody deserves murder, and she hadn't been just anybody. She had been beautiful and she had been sweet. More than that, I couldn't shake off the conviction that she had gone into her murderer's hands only because of me. It wasn't only that he had killed her because she'd left him for me, it was that she had put herself in the way of it because she had been afraid for me.

I couldn't leave it alone. She had given her life for mine. It didn't matter that she had in all probability never had the thought that she would be giving it. She had done it for me, and now she was dead of it. The police were looking for the two men and they were looking for John Gibbs, and they might even find them. I had given them all the information I had and their resources were far greater than mine, but I couldn't sit back and just let them take it on. I wanted to find the three of them, and, above all, I wanted to find John Gibbs. I owed that much to myself and I owed it to those days and nights I'd had with Barbie. They had been good days and good nights, and now it hurt to remember them. That hurt was demanding that I find John Gibbs. I'd turn him over to the gendarmes, but first I wanted him for myself.

His two men meant much less to me, but if I could catch up with them, they might lead me to him. I was going to make them do just that. I must admit I had no plans—I was going ahead on nothing but pain and rage and determination. Some way I was going to do it. When the time came, I was going to find a way.

That didn't make much sense, but rage never does make much sense, and pain makes none at all. They just spur a man to action, and the odds are good that it will be foolish action.

It was a long drive over those secondary roads, and it was almost noon when we came into Perros-Guirec. I checked into a beach hotel. It was the kind of hotel I would have chosen for her. I hoped it was the sort of hotel where they would come looking for me, because I was going to be waiting for them.

While I waited, I put in a stupid day. I had some kind of lunch and some kind of dinner. Ordinarily eating in France, I am aware of what I'm eating, but that day I was just taking on fuel. In between I walked the town, walked and watched. It was no good looking for their car. They had dumped it, but I was looking for them. I went from café to café, the ones along the plage, the little ones in the back streets. In café after café I sat and watched and I drank calvados.

Do you know calvados? The Normans make it out of apples. The nearest thing to it is Jersey lightning, but stacked up against calvados, even the most potent applejack is feeble stuff, and by the same comparison the smoothest applejack is rough.

I don't know how many I had, but all through the afternoon and deep into the night it was just about nonstop. It should have knocked me on my tail, but all the way I never felt that it was doing anything to me. My rage seemed to be soaking it up. I never for a moment felt anything but cold sober.

When the last of the cafés shut down—it was a laborers' zinc down a back street—I walked and I walked. Mathilda was at my heels all the time. The streets were deserted. All the shops and cafés were shuttered. There wasn't a lighted window anywhere, and everything was silent. I was hearing nothing but my own footfalls, and I was seeing nothing.

Maybe it was the calvados finally getting to me or maybe it was simple exhaustion. I had been feeling as though I would never sleep again, but suddenly that changed. I felt I could sleep. I headed for the hotel. I was trying to think of something I could do next. I had wasted the day. Prowling Perros-Guirec had brought me nothing. I promised myself that I would think about it in the morning. I would have to come up with some better ideas, something like an intelligent plan.

The hotel was all buttoned up for the night. I should have rung for the porter, but I was remembering the hotel at Mont St. Michel and that entrance from the battlements that was never locked. Here, of course, there were no battlements. Nevertheless, it occurred to me that here, too, there might be no need for waking the night man.

There was the hotel garden. I had a ground-floor room that opened directly to the garden. There was a row of such rooms. If I could locate the one that was mine, and if no maid had been in to lock the french doors I had left open because I liked having the smells of garden and sea air in the room, I could just walk in from the garden and disturb no one.

I tried it but, once I was in the garden, I began having doubts. All the doors looked alike and all were uniformly shut. I'd made no count before leaving the hotel. I knew that mine was not one of the end rooms. I remembered it as being somewhere in the middle of the row, but whether it was the third from the left or the fourth or the fifth I didn't know. In any event, the doors had been shut. I was assuming that they had been locked.

I was about to turn back and ring for the night concierge when Mathilda took over. Unerringly she headed for the fourth pair of french doors. Rearing up, she planted her forepaws against the glass. The door swung in and Mathilda went trotting into the room. I followed after her. The doors had only been shut. They hadn't been locked. The maid had been in and turned down the bed. When I followed Mathilda into the room, I found the dog already settled on the bed.

It seemed to me that she had the right idea. I plunked myself down beside her. I should have thought that there were differences between the two of us. Mathilda had no clothes to take off, but if I had the thought, I didn't act on it. The calvados had taken over. I must have gone right to sleep.

Let's not mince words. I fell straight into a drunken stupor, dreamless, totally insensate. I woke to total darkness and total headache. I also woke to nausea and a feeling of motion. Have you ever gone to bed with a skinful? Can you remember lying there and wishing that the bed would settle down and hold still? Have you ever felt your gorge rise at the stink of the stale alcohol on your own breath?

There's a couple of times in the course of a misspent life

that I'd had it like that. In my first moments of waking I just told myself that here it was again.

"This too will pass away," I was thinking.

Almost immediately, however, I began having other thoughts. In all my earlier experiences of beds that wouldn't hold still there had been this same swaying motion, but it had always been silent. There had been no slapping sounds, no creaking, and nothing like a throbbing chug-chug. There was also the stink. It wasn't a stale smell, and I'd never known alcohol, fresh or stale, to smell like that.

I concentrated on the smell. I don't know how long it might have been before I identified it if I had not had the feeling that my arms and legs were cramped. I tried to stretch them and I found I couldn't. Things began sorting themselves out.

My arms were tied down to my sides and I was also bound at ankles and knees. Even in the moment that I was recognizing that, I came clear on the smell. I wasn't stinking of alcohol, or, if I was, that smell was lost in the overwhelming stench of chloroform. Having that established, I put my mind to the swaying and the sounds. I wasn't long coming clear on those as well. I was on a boat. I was below decks. The throbbing I felt was the boat engine. The swaying was the motion of the sea. The sounds were boat-engine sounds and they were the slapping of waves against the boat's planking.

I was lying flat on my back and there was a weight on my chest. I tried to bring my hands up to push it off, but I couldn't move my arms. I could only flex my fingers. I did what I could. I brought my head forward. My chin brushed something soft and warm and velvety. I knew what that was. I was brushing against one of Mathilda's long, floppy ears.

I whispered her name.

"Mathilda."

I expected I'd feel her tongue slurp against my face. I expected I'd feel the motion of her hindquarters with the wagging of her tail. I've told you about her tail wag. Hers was always a case of the tail wagging the dog.

I felt none of that. She just lay there on my chest, inert, a dead weight. I strained against my bonds. My first thought was filling me up with horror and rage. They had killed the dog and dumped her body onto me. I tried to do a situp, but I made it only partway before my head hit hard and I was stopped. I had gone far enough, however, to roll the dog's body down off my chest. It now lay across my belly, but the dog hadn't moved. It was only that, by rearing up, I had moved her.

In her new position, however, her muzzle was up against my left hand. I felt her breath warm and moist against my fingers. It was some time before the meaning of it came through to me. The dog wasn't dead. She was just out cold. Now that I had her off my chest, the stench of the chloroform wasn't gone, but it was diminished. I figured that out. Now I was smelling it only on my own breath. I was no longer smelling it on hers. So that was it. We had both been chloroformed.

I was thinking in bitterness that I had been easy, but I wondered about Mathilda. I remembered that at one time during the evening I had dipped my finger into one of my unnumbered snorts of calvados and let her lick the stuff off my hand. I was certain that she'd had no more than a drop or two. I remembered times when we had been with Barbie and Mathilda'd had a taste of Barbie's drink as well as of mine. Those drops had never had any effect on her. I'm not saying that she's a pup who can hold her liquor, but she'd never had enough to make even a baby drunk, and that night she'd had only half as much as she'd licked off our fingers on those other occasions.

It seemed impossible that she hadn't barked and raised a fuss to rouse the whole hotel, but then I remembered her the way she had been that first time at Mont St. Michel. She hadn't barked then. She'd growled. She'd whimpered. She'd bitten. I wondered if the old adage could be turned around.

Biting dogs don't bark.

I had time to think, and after a little I was reminding myself that this kind of thinking would get me nowhere. Thinking about what had been was futile. I needed to think about what was going to be. We had been pulled out of the hotel and we were being taken out to sea.

When they had grabbed Barbie and trussed her up the way they now had me trussed up, we'd thought of it as nothing more than her man wanting her back and sending his goons to bring her back by force. Then later, on the battlements of the Château Gaillard, there had been reason to question that assumption. There they had been trying to knock *me* off. What did that mean?

One way of figuring it had been that their orders had been changed.

"Grab her and bring her back to me, but first kill that bastard who took her away."

The other way would have been that, on their experience at Mont St. Michel, they had learned that they weren't going to take her from me without a fight. Having no appetite for a fight, they had tried to do it the easy way. They would bump Erridge off and, with him out of the way, they could grab the girl. But now Barbie was dead and I was wondering whether that hadn't been in the program all along. Their orders had been to kidnap her and bring her back to the boss. He wanted to kill her with his own two hands.

I said there was no good in thinking about what had been, but I couldn't get away from it. What had been held the only clues I could have to what was going to be. He'd had her back and he'd killed her. So now what would he want with me?

It could be as it had been with Barbie. He needed the pleasure of killing me with his own two hands. Then there was Mathilda. They had chloroformed her and brought her along. I was trying to understand that. I was asking myself what they could want with the pup. There was, of course, the one she had run off down the road. She'd had her teeth into that one. Maybe the head man had a score to settle with Erridge, and his goon had one to settle with Mathilda.

That, it seemed to me, would be too far out, but then, again, these guys were far out. I wasn't ready to put any sort of nonsense past them, not so long as it was vicious nonsense. They were taking us out to sea. I began seeing pictures of a concrete block tied to my feet and another tied to Mathilda's. Man and dog disappear without a trace. Nobody takes too much trouble looking for them. He's just another hotel guest who's skipped his bill. That could explain their taking Mathilda. A guy doesn't skip his hotel bill and not take his dog with him.

I got that far, and then I remembered Baby. A guy doesn't skip his hotel bill and leave his Porsche and his luggage behind him. It could be that they hadn't thought of that. On past performance I knew that they were stupid. Not the head man, of course. On past performance this John Gibbs was a smart operator. It was just his goons who weren't bright.

My picture of the concrete blocks and the heave overboard wouldn't go away, but all the time I was lying there and thinking, I was also listening. The sounds were constant—the throbbing chug of the engine, the creaking of the boat's timbers, and the slap of the waves. Now and again, however, there were other sounds. I heard a tolling bell. Sometime later I heard a deep-toned whistle. It sounded in a pattern of toots, and the pattern repeated again and again, louder as we approached it, fading off as we moved away from it.

I thought about those sounds. They weren't boat sounds. They were buoy sounds, a bell buoy, a whistling buoy. Those sounds meant something. We had been so long on the water—I was counting only conscious time, since I didn't know how long I had been unconscious and afloat—that the buoys had to mean that we weren't headed away from the shore. We were following the coast, staying reasonably close in. I thought about that and, with the thought, my picture of the concrete blocks began to fade. I had wanted to meet up with this John Gibbs, and I was about to have my wish. I would be having it and it wouldn't be good. This was hardly the way I'd wanted it, not this way, trussed up and helpless.

I thought of shouting to see what that would bring me. I wasn't gagged. I had my voice. That meant something too. We were out in a boat, away from everybody and everything. I could yell my head off and it wasn't going to bring anybody. At least it would bring nobody but my captors, and I could wait for them to come to me in their own good time. I could do myself no good by hurrying it. I needed all the time they would be giving me. I needed it for all this thinking I had to do, not that I was doing any that was taking me anywhere.

Then he came. I heard the thud of his feet on the deck overhead and I heard him as he came below. The cabin door slammed open and I could see nothing but the bulk of him silhouetted against a faint light, but that was only for a moment. He hit a switch and the cabin lights came on. I recognized him. He was one of the two I'd had a good look at that night at Mont St. Michel. One of his hands was bandaged and, with the lights on, I could see a smear of blood dried on Mathilda's muzzle.

It was the lug she had chased down the causeway. Evidently she'd sunk her teeth into him again. That one had no luck with Mathilda. He was carrying something in his bandaged hand. It was white, but beyond that I couldn't figure what it was.

He came up to the bunk and started working at it. It was a roll of adhesive tape. He stripped a good length off the roll. Grabbing a double handful of Mathilda's ears, he pulled her head up and pressed one end of the tape under the dog's chin. Then he wound the tape around and around, improvising a sort of muzzle.

"Don't get it too tight," I said. "Let her breathe."

He went on winding tape.

"It won't bug me none if she chokes herself," he said.

Having finished with Mathilda, he turned to me. I was telling myself that I shouldn't have been thinking about a gag. It was crazy, but I was having the notion that just having had the thought in my mind had put it into his head.

He tried to slap a length of tape on my lips. I rolled my head away from it. Muttering curses, he grabbed my ear with his bandaged hand. I fought it so hard that I felt as though I was tearing my ear off, but he hung with it and he got the tape on tight over my mouth.

"Now," he said, "you won't bite either and you won't talk till we're ready for you."

I was only half listening to him. My mind was on his bandaged hand. Working with it, he had done it no good.

Fresh blood was soaking through his bandage. Following my gaze, he looked down at the hand. Cursing some more, he snapped off the cabin light and went out, slamming the door shut behind him. I was wishing he'd left it open. I wanted that little light that had been coming through it, and I wanted the air. Even in the few minutes he'd been in the cabin with the door open behind him, some of the reek of the chloroform had thinned out. I would have liked to be rid of the rest of it.

What seemed like a long time passed, but finally Mathilda came out of the chloroform. She stirred, and almost at once she began pawing at her taped muzzle, trying to work the tape off. By the feel of her weight on me, I knew that she was sitting up on her haunches. I could feel one of her forepaws braced against me and the up-and-down motion of the other paw. Even though in the dark I couldn't see what she was trying to do, it was an easy guess.

I wished she'd get back down to lie across my belly the way she'd been. I had the use of my fingers. If she would only bring her muzzle down to where it had been against my hand, I could have gotten a grip on the tape and worked it off.

I spoke to her. I told her to lie down. They'd taught her that at obedience school, to lie down on command, but they hadn't taught her that the command meant she was to lie across a guy's belly.

Obviously I couldn't get the words out past the tape on my own mouth, but I did manage some muffled noises and Mathilda responded to them. She moved up on the bunk. She nuzzled my face. It was the nearest she could come to licking it. It wasn't her fault that she didn't have the use of her tongue. She was doing her best. She stayed there and she tried to work her tape off. There was nothing I could do to get her back down to where I could get my fingers on it.

VII.

We were stuck there that way for what seemed like the better part of forever. I couldn't see my watch. I tried to measure the passing time by counting seconds. Somewhere around two thousand I gave up on that. I felt that what I was doing amounted to taking a count on the throbbing in my head. Maybe it wasn't making that throbbing worse, but it seemed as though it was. Two thousand would have been about a half hour or possibly a few minutes more, but I felt as though I'd been a much longer time counting it up. I told myself that minutes were ticking away at their usual pace. They just seemed much slower to me. It was no good even trying to estimate it.

One thing became more and more certain. We weren't being taken out to sea to be murdered by drowning. We had been on the water too long a time for that. We were being taken somewhere, but I couldn't even make a guess at where. We were following the coast. I kept hearing the sounds that verified it. It wasn't only the buoys. Periodically there would also be a change in the water sounds, a surging roar and a crash. I could identify that. It would be the water breaking against rocks. I was thinking that a veteran boatman with a veteran's knowledge of that Breton shoreline might have known where he was. He would know which buoy threw out which signal and at just what points the beaches gave way to a rockbound shore.

I had done some sailing at one time or another but never

out of Perros-Guirec, and never enough to have learned to know the buoys without reference to the charts. At one point Mathilda hopped down off the bunk. I could hear her padding around the cabin and I could hear the wheeze of her labored breathing. With her muzzle taped up the way it was, the sound of her breathing came through something like a muffled whistle.

Then she was making another sound along with it. It was a rattling, scraping sound. She was scratching at the closed cabin door. After a considerable time she gave up on that and, except for the wheezing and a small hissing noise, she was quiet.

She was a good dog. She had tried her best. It wasn't her fault. She couldn't have been expected to hold it forever. I lay there approving of her and hoping that she was making a great mess. They were going to have to clean it up.

Maybe I'm suggestible or maybe it was just that it had been a long time and I had taken a lot of calvados aboard. Mathilda came back onto the bunk and resumed her futile efforts at her tape. I hoped she would settle at a spot where I could reach it, but she didn't. She lay at my feet and swiped at her tape down there.

Meanwhile I had another problem. I was in as bad shape as Mathilda had been. The memory of an encounter I'd once had with an Englishman in the loo of an Oxford pub popped into my head.

"We don't buy our drink," he said. "We only rent it."

I'd rented an incalculable quantity of calvados, and expiration time on the lease had caught up with me. I worked up a great sweat fighting it, but inevitably it was a losing battle. I wet the bed.

I suppose, because I was preoccupied with that, I was slow to notice the change in the boat sounds. The slapping of the water against the planking had stopped and with it the swaying motion. There was still the throb and chugging of the engine but now it was throttled down. We had made port and we were slowed, gliding along through smooth water. I waited and listened. There was nothing else I could do. I heard the engine cut out and then I heard running feet overhead. A jolting bump came near to pitching Mathilda and me out of the bunk. Then something banged against the planking over my head. There was also some shouting up there. Obviously we were coming into a mooring. I braced myself for what would be coming next, but nothing came.

I was beginning to think that they had just put in for fuel or provisions and that we would be heading out again. I wondered about the possibility of the long run westward and around past Brest and then south for an eventual landing somewhere along the coast of Spain. It didn't strike me as too far-fetched to figure that, after killing the girl, Gibbs had skipped the country to hole up across the Spanish border and wait there for his boys to bring me to him.

Since I couldn't think ahead, I got to fretting about what seemed to be more immediate problems. That was going to be a long journey. I fell to worrying about Mathilda. For her it would be too long without food or water, and yet I couldn't see how they could remove the tape without coming down with yet another case of dog bite.

The tape they had on my mouth they could handle. Here in port they couldn't risk letting me yell. There would be the danger that I might be heard, but once we were out at sea again and away from other boats, they'd have no need to worry about that. That, of course, was not saying that they would bother to give me food or water; but, if they chose to, it would be possible.

Fresh sounds came at me and knocked off all this thinking. There was the thud of feet overhead and the cabin door opened. This time sunlight came flooding in, and this time there were three of them silhouetted in the doorway. They came down into the cabin dragging behind them a big wicker hamper. It was one of those square, covered jobs.

You don't see them in the States, and even in Europe they're not as common as they once were. People once used them when moving. They were great for household stuff like blankets and pillows and eiderdowns. I didn't have to do much thinking about what they were about to pack in this one. They couldn't lug me ashore in broad daylight without attracting too much unwelcome notice, not the way they had me all trussed up. The thing was big enough. They could cram me down into it.

I was thinking about the three men. Two of them I knew. I had tangled with that pair at Mont St. Michel. The third was a new face. It wasn't Barbie's Johnny. It wasn't even his type or the type of the two goons. This one was far smoother.

He was young and he was big and burly, but he was smooth. I was guessing him for about twenty-five or possibly a year or two less, certainly no more. He had the build of an athlete in top shape, but he had the look and the bearing of one of those young guys you might see around a bank, the type who is fated to go far.

He was also dressed for the part, not the banker's correct business suit but what the correct young banker would wear for leisure. His beautiful canary-colored slacks were gleamingly immaculate and in impeccable press. His white bucks showed just that subtle bit of soil that is required if a man would proclaim himself as not so crass as to be caught wearing brand-new shoes. His black knit shirt showed the mark of one of those Rue de Fauborg St. Honoré dress designers who has discovered that there is good hunting in the men's fashion business.

His hair was the correctly fashionable length and it had been blown dry. He had the kind of expensive suntan that is acquired by long, casual exposure to the sun but only in the best places. There was none of the weatherbeaten look of the working stiff whose job takes him out in all kinds of weather, and there was none of the blackening that shows in a tan that has been rushed along because there's only a two-week vacation in which to get it done.

He didn't look tough. His face was something of a contradiction of his size and his muscles. The face was almost girlish. He wasn't even trying to look tough. Anything I could read in his expression was superior, supercilious, and contemptuous. He had the look of a guy who was dealing with his inferiors and doing his best to mask his disgust. He baffled me. Everything about him seemed to be wrong for a guy in the John Gibbs entourage.

It was obvious, however, that he was the man in command. He stood back, taking a supervisory stance, while the two lugs went to work. They came over to the bunk and reached for me. There wasn't much I could do, but I did what I could. I thrashed about. I brought my knees up and with my two feet I got in a good kick on one of them. That one fell back.

The third one came forward. He held up his fist. He wasn't doing anything with it. He was just showing it to me. As a fist, it wasn't bad. He had big, heavy hands and a fighter's thick wrists. That, however, was not what he was exhibiting for my benefit. His hand wasn't bare. It had fitted to it a shiny set of brass knucks.

"I suggest that you behave yourself, Erridge," he said. "If you're troublesome, you will only make it rough on yourself. You're going to behave and you're going to talk.

We will see to that. If we have to do it the hard way, it will only be by your choice, and I promise you this. It won't be hard on us. It will be hard on you."

It was cultivated speech, possibly even something on the prissy side. It was also confusing. I was going to talk. What the hell did I have to talk about? What made it even more confusing was a feeling I had that I knew the voice or, if not the voice, the accent, the way of talking. I wasted no time trying to think that one out. I knew that I'd never seen the man before.

Meanwhile Mathilda was having her troubles. She went charging at one of the guys and then another. She was doing her best to sink her teeth into them, but of course she couldn't. She was the perfect picture of desperate frustration and she had my sympathy. She looked the way I felt.

"Nobody's going to hurt you unless you make it necessary," his nibs continued. "We are just going to move you to a place where there can be no interference and where, if you co-operate, we can make you more comfortable. I should think you would welcome the opportunity to get out of your wet pants and to have the tape off your mouth. All that's required of you is that you tell us where he is, and you can't do that till we have moved you to a place where we can allow you to talk. You won't be too cramped in the hamper and it won't be for long. So now let's come along quietly. After all, Erridge, it's all in the game, and you must recognize that you've lost. Isn't it time for you to be a good loser?"

Somebody was crazy and I wasn't at all certain that the somebody wasn't Erridge. I was trying to work it out every which way, and there was no way I could bring it around to where it even began to make sense. One thing I could understand. I was clean out of choices. I was going to go along quietly. Whether it would be because I was being co-operative or because he would have used his pacifier on me, I would be going along.

Pride was telling me to fight it; good sense was telling me I had nothing to fight with. I could see nothing for it but to take this guy at his word. Maybe, as he put it, they would make me more comfortable. Maybe that would mean I would be untied. Maybe then I could do something effective. If such a moment was ever going to come, I wanted to meet it as far as possible undamaged. Just in case, I had to give myself the best chance of being effective.

I relaxed. I let them pick me up and fold me into the hamper. Before they could get the lid down, Mathilda jumped in with me. She landed on top of me. One of them reached in for her. It was the one with the undamaged hand. The guy with the bandage had had enough of her.

"Leave her," the man in charge said.

"What for?" bandaged hand asked. "Who wants the mutt?"

"He wants her," his nibs said. "He won't like watching her being hurt. We might need her to get him to talk."

With that he shut the lid down on Mathilda and me. Mathilda reared up against it, but it didn't budge. It had been secured. It was a bumpy ride while they wrestled the hamper up onto the deck and brought it ashore. We were loaded into something, a truck or a station wagon. I had no way of knowing.

I felt the motion. I heard the grinding of the gears. I felt the sway when we took a couple of turns. I remembered stories I'd read about guys in a spot like this. They knew by the sway whether a turn was to the left or the right. They counted turns. They were alert to significant sounds, the bell and the bumping that meant a railroad crossing, children singing in ragged chorus that meant they were passing a school, the bang of jackhammers that meant a road excavation, stuff like that.

Maybe it can be done. I don't know. If I'd had any clue to what town I was in, if I knew just where on the waterfront I'd been loaded off the boat, if it was a town I knew well enough to have a map of it in my head, maybe I could have done it. As it was, however, I would have been operating without any base. I didn't even make a try at it.

Also, I had something else to occupy me. Folded into that hamper the way I was with Mathilda crunched down on top of me, I found myself finally having what I'd wanted through those hours on the boat. Her muzzle was touching my right hand. I had the tape right under my fingers. Exploring with my fingertips, I found the end of it. It was wrinkled. Mathilda had accomplished that much with all her pawing. Scratching at it, I worked it loose and I was able to get a grip on it. I started to unwind it. It was slow and laborious. The amount of play I had for my hand was limited. I could work it free maybe only a few centimeters at a time. Then, when I'd pulled away a couple of inches of tape, its loose end, flapping about, attached itself afresh to the poor pup's hide.

That had to be worked loose and it couldn't be done without pulling on Mathilda's hair. Her yelp was muffled but it was a yelp of pain. If I'd had more freedom of movement, I could have given it a quick yank, but I couldn't manage anything better than a slow pull. If you've ever been taped up, you know how hard that was on her. I got it loose and, rolling it between my fingers, buried the adhesive surface inside the roll and went back to loosening tape. Now, however, even while I was loosening it, I was rolling it in, leaving nothing to flap about and latch back onto Mathilda.

I was doing well with it, but time and again I had to

stop because my fingers cramped and went useless. Each time that happened, I worked at flexing them until they were loosened up enough to go back to work. We had picked up speed. I could feel that we were rolling along at a good clip. I could figure that much even though it was giving me no clue to where we were or where we were going.

He had said they were taking me to a place where I could talk and he would have no worry about interference. It was reasonable that this should have been a place away from the town, whatever town it had been where we'd made our landing. It would be out of the country, someplace so far isolated from neighbors or passers-by that I could yell my head off and there would be nobody to hear.

Each time I worked the cramp out of my fingers and returned to picking at the tape, I had a shorter interval before the cramp set back in. After much sweat I had it down to the place where there was nothing holding the dog's muzzle but the innermost layer of tape. I had no more than started on that before I discovered that it had been all for nothing.

We were down to the slow, torturing pull on hair and in a most sensitive area, those tender places around the mouth. Mathilda gave out with another of those muffled yelps, and there was going to be no way I could shorten the prolonged agony for her.

She took care of that herself. She squirmed and rolled in the cramped space, and she got her head out of reach of my fingers. With my own mouth taped shut, I couldn't talk to her, not that I was kidding myself that talk could have been any help. I would need to have had both my hands free and probably the help of another pair of hands to hold her while I pulled the tape off in one quick yank. It was hopeless. I had nothing.

I was just down to riding along and cursing. It was, I suppose, better than sniveling, but that's the most I can say for it. I felt the sway. It was a right turn and then we were on a change of surface. It was no longer the hiss of tires on paved road. It was a crunch. We were on gravel. I braced myself for what would be coming now. This had to be a private driveway. I had encountered no road in the whole Normandy and Brittany area, no matter how minor a back road it might have been, that wasn't paved.

Riding along on the gravel, I felt turn after turn, and it was stretching into a long ride. This, then, would be a big place, no villa that sat with only a couple of acres around it. I visualized something more like a château, something surrounded by acres of formal garden bedded deep in a wooded park. From what the flics had told me, it had been evident that Barbie's Johnny Gibbs was one of the big-time crooks, but this seemed to be too much. I hadn't imagined that he could be anything like this big-time.

We came to a stop. I heard the tailgate come down. I could guess it was a station wagon or, at most, a small panel truck. Our hamper was wrestled out of the thing and dropped to the gravel. We sat there for a time while they stood over the hamper and argued. I could recognize the three voices and differentiate them.

The two lugs wanted to haul me out of the hamper and untie my legs so that they could frog-march me into the house. The big smoothie was vetoing that idea. He was telling them that they were being paid for muscle, and on past performance they hadn't been giving nearly enough to earn their pay.

"I'll do the thinking," he said. "You just pick that thing up and carry it inside."

I heard them grumble, but orders were orders. They picked up the hamper and carried it with us still in it.

There were a few moments of tilt while they were evidently mounting a flight of maybe five or six steps. Then it was a stretch on the level where I could hear the bang of their heels against the floor. I was guessing hardwood or maybe marble.

When they set the hamper down, I was braced for the lid coming up, expecting that the time had come when they would be hauling us out of the thing. The lid didn't come up. They did something baffling instead. They shoved the hamper, sliding it along the floor.

That was followed by a moment or two of nothing. I was beginning to think that they had shoved us into some sort of closet and were just going to leave us there, but then I felt a new kind of motion. We were rising. Since we started up with a jerk, I did feel it. That meant an elevator, and that made the deal even more big-time.

I couldn't imagine a country hotel. It had to be some big son-of-a-gun of a modern country house or an old château that had been expensively modernized. The big, old jobs come on the market from time to time and, even if they are in an advanced state of ruin, they command a heavy price. A man has to be prepared to pay and pay and pay if he wants to then make the place livable, not to speak of installing any such frills as an elevator. I had begun to think upper bracket. Now I was revising it to top bracket.

The thing jerked to a stop. I had no way of estimating how many stories we had risen. It had seemed like a long ascent, but the jobs they install in even the most palatial private dwellings are not express elevators. All of those I've ever known just ooze slowly up or down. I made a guess at a couple of stories. It could have been as many as four, but in a place where the ceilings were high, two or three would have been more likely.

For quite a bit we just stayed there with nothing happening. Then I heard doors opening, and with it I was hearing something else. It was the two goons again. They were still grumbling, but now they were breathing hard. It was easy putting that together.

Those private-house elevators are small. One big enough to have taken the hamper would have been larger than average. Big enough to take even one man along with the hamper would have been impossibly outsize. They had loaded us in and had sent us up while they had to run up the stairs. The boss man was making them do this the hard way.

They slid the hamper out of the elevator and then they picked it up and carried it again. That carry was only a short distance. They dropped it and for a while nothing happened and there was no sound but their grumbling and panting plus a sound of soft moaning. My first thought was that they had taken other prisoners and they had brought us here to join their other captives, who would be lying there helpless, unable to do anything but moan.

I listened to the moaning. I was trying to find some shape of words in it. I could find none. A picture came to me—row on row of guys like myself, all with their lips taped up, incapable of articulating anything at all.

One of the goons took up a fresh theme for his grumbling.

"Them goddamn pigeons," he said.

It was a disproportionate relief, or maybe it wasn't disproportionate. I had been so long unable to make sense of anything that to have even so small an item explain itself in a way that wasn't preposterous handed me a small return of confidence in my sanity.

We would be in a tower room or someplace like that up

under a mansard roof where doves were nesting in the eaves. It's the sound they make. They're not called mourning doves for nothing.

We were waiting and I wondered what for. I was listening for the sound of the boss man's voice, but from what the other two were saying it became obvious that he wasn't with us.

"It burns me taking all that lip from the snotty fag," one of them said.

"They're all like that," said the other.

"What do you think he's doing now?"

"Combing his hair. He's always combing his hair."

I heard another sound, and with it they shut up. This one I knew. It was the elevator door opening and shutting. I could work that out. These two had been sent running up the stairs to haul the hamper out of the elevator and send the car back down for his nibs. He'd been waiting down below till he could ride up.

"All right," he said. "Don't just sit around. We haven't got forever. Open that thing up and get him out of there."

The lid came up and Mathilda growled. Not much sound of it was coming through, but I could feel the rumble of it in her body where she was pressed against me. They picked her off me and dumped her on the floor. They were getting a grip on me, but they had to give it up when Mathilda jumped right back in and landed on top of me.

His nibs laughed. He shouldered his goons aside and picking up the squirming dog, he held her. He stood back, stroking her.

"Come on," he said. "Be a good dog."

My guesses hadn't been bad. It was an attic room, but high ceilinged under the mansard roof. There were a couple of doves perched on the sill of the dormer window. I could see that much past the two lugs who were manhandling me out of the hamper. They got me up out of it, but then they didn't set me down. They just dropped me, and they grinned at the thud I made hitting the floor.

"Get the tape off his mouth, or are you afraid he'll bite too?" the head man said.

"He goddamn better not," the one with the bandaged hand muttered.

He stood back and left it to the other man to yank off the tape, but it wasn't too far back, just in a good position for aiming a kick at my groin. He wasn't pulling the trigger on that kick. He was just holding it there in case I showed a sign of turning vicious.

The other guy squatted down beside me, carefully setting himself where he wouldn't be obstructing the kick. He planted the flat of his left hand against my face, covering my forehead and my eyes and holding my head down tight against the floorboards. With his right he got a fingernail under a corner of the tape and slowly lifted enough of it so that he could grip it between his thumb and forefinger.

Slowly and slowly he pulled it away. On any estimate, it had been more than forty-eight hours since I had last shaved. That had been in the morning at the hotel in Vernon. Ordinarily I would have shaved again that day before dinner, or at least before bedtime. I'm a two-shaves-a-day man most days when I'm in any civilized place, and anytime that I'm not sleeping alone.

You know what the night of that day was like. I got no dinner and it was obvious that I was going to be sleeping alone. I'd had no thought of shaving then, and in the morning in St. Brieuc I skipped it again. I was seeing nothing coming up at me that day that was going to ask for a smooth chin. Now I was well into the day after that. The night had seemed interminably long, but I didn't think I'd been trussed up on that boat more than overnight.

In more than forty-eight hours I sprout a sizable stubble. I'm not saying that around the muzzle I was as hairy as Mathilda; but if I hadn't known it then, I was now learning what had made her yelp when I tried to work on that last layer of tape.

Since he wouldn't jerk the damn thing off, I tried to do it. A quick turn of my head while he had his grip on the tape would have done it, but he had my head pinned tight against the floor with most of his weight behind it. I couldn't move it. I had to stay there while he squeezed every last ounce of torture out of freeing my mouth.

Meanwhile fancy pants was talking to me and I had to work at listening.

"You're a stupid bastard," he was saying, "but it looks like you've begun to get smart. Stay that way and you'll get out of this easy. I guess you know how close you came to getting this bitch shot."

He was looking at the last layer of tape wrapped around Mathilda's snoot. He was talking about that. The way he was reading it, I had worked at restoring Mathilda to biting condition, but at the last moment I had thought better of it. He was thinking that I'd realized that if I'd freed her jaws and she had come out of the hamper with her teeth bared and ready to sink into the first hand that reached into the hamper, they would have killed the pup.

Listening to him, I was telling myself that I should have thought of that, but I wasn't about to tell him that I hadn't.

"Take it off her," I said.

He laughed.

"You think I'm crazy? If you want if off her, you're going to take it off, you and nobody else."

"Untie me and let me have her."

"You think you can control her?"

"I can as long as nobody touches me. She's a good dog."

"If you can't control her, she'll be a dead dog."

"I'll control her."

"And what if we have to touch you? You know. Slap you around? Kick you where it counts? Put the squeeze on the crown jewels?"

"Not then," I said. "They didn't teach her anything like that in obedience school."

"We'll have to remember that," he said.

"Much as you may enjoy it," I said, "you may not have to slap me around. I don't know what you want me to tell you, but once you start asking questions, you'll find I have no secrets."

"Maybe you have been getting smart," he said. "Where is he?"

"Where's who?"

He sighed.

"It was too much to ask," he said. "You haven't been getting smart."

"Untie me and let me get the tape off the dog," I said. "We'll get along better then."

"Okay," he said. "Wait. I won't be a minute."

With that he trotted out of the room. I made a try with the goons.

"What's all this about?" I asked.

"Shut up," the one with the bandaged hand said.

"He wants me to talk," I said. "Someone's going to have to tell me what we're talking about."

"He pretends like he doesn't know," the other one said.

"There's only one thing wrong with that," I said. "I *don't* know."

"Then you'll have to learn."

"That's what I'm waiting for."

"Yeah," bandaged hand said. "We're waiting, too. We'll learn you."

Canary pants came trotting back. He was making no secret of what he'd gone for. He came carrying it in his hand. It was a revolver, the heavy artillery kind, a .45. His bully boys were both wearing shoulder holsters, but apparently he didn't consider them too dependable. I could understand why. He leveled his artillery piece at me.

"Untie his hands," he said.

They were taking no chances with me. The lug who came over to untie me chose his angle of approach carefully. Not for even a moment was he obstructing the .45's line of fire.

He freed my hands. I needed a little time for flexing them to get the stiffness out of them and to restore circulation. Mathilda was huddled up against me, taking weary and futile paw swipes at the tape on her nose. When the man had gone out to pick up the gun, he'd let go of her and she'd dashed right to me.

I stroked her and talked to her.

"Well," the man said. "Get it off her."

"I'll need a solvent," I said.

"We didn't need a solvent for you. Take it off."

"Then, someone will have to hold her," I said.

The man looked to his two henchmen. The one with the bandaged hand backed off. The man switched to the other one. The lug shook his head.

"You do it," he said. "That's a wild mutt."

"Oh, nuts," fancy pants said. "You two big, brave kids keep me covered. Shoot if you have to, but don't shoot the bitch. We'll need her. And don't shoot to kill. A slug in his arm or his shoulder or his leg will do it. You think, if you try real hard, you can remember that he hasn't talked yet?"

They pulled their guns out of their shoulder holsters.

"Maybe if you didn't talk so much," one of them said.

"Maybe if you hadn't let him take the girl away from you," canary slacks came back at them.

He set his gun on the windowsill. With a whirring of wings the two doves flew off. Circling around out of the line of fire, he came to me and squatted down beside me. He got a good grip on Mathilda.

"I'm holding her," he said. "Pull it off."

For that moment the three of them were together. They all three broke out grins that were so alike that they could have swapped faces and nobody'd ever have known the difference. It was a moment of joy for them. They were going to watch me hurt the poor pup, and they were going to see her sink her teeth in my hand.

I stroked her beautiful long ears and I whispered into them. I was telling her that it was going to be only a moment of pain and she was going to feel ever so much better after it. I was telling her how sorry I was, but that there was no other way of doing it and she knew as well as I did that she had to have that cruel tape off.

Don't think I was hoping she'd understand the words, but I did hope that maybe something in the tone of my voice would get through to her.

"Oh, come on," the man said. "Quit stalling. Rip it off."

I took a good grip and put everything I had into giving it a quick, hard yank. Mathilda yelped with pain and whipped her head around at my hand. She came at it with her teeth bared, but even in the moment that she had my hand between her teeth, she pulled back. She licked my hand. I grabbed her away from fancy pants and held her tight against me. Her tail began to wag.

"Okay," the guy said. "Now talk."

At the sound of his voice Mathilda whipped around toward him and growled.

He jumped back out of range.

"Hold her," he yipped. "Control her."

"Down, Mathilda," I said. "Good dog. Down."

She watched his retreat. Then, satisfied that he was keeping his distance, she took her baleful gaze off him and turned back to me.

The man retrieved his gun from the windowsill.

"I've got him," he told his lugs. "Put your guns away."

Evidently he had no confidence in their aim. He preferred to rely on his own.

"What do you want to know?" I asked.

"Where have you got him?"

"Look," I said. "We're getting nowhere. That's the same question in different words, and I still don't know who you're talking about except that I haven't got anybody."

"Don't give me that. You know what I mean. The rest of your gang, you, it's the same thing."

"I haven't a gang either. Just tell me who you're talking about and maybe we can take it from there."

"All right," he said. "If you want to play games, I'll play along this far, but don't think my patience will go on forever. Mr. Elston. Where have you got him?"

VIII.

I should have come up with a quick answer, but when that kind of question comes at you out of nowhere, you just have no answers. You're all tied up with trying to guess what kind of game you're in. So I was slow with my reply. The inevitable assumption was that I had taken the time to think up a lie.

"The last time I saw Elston," I said, "he was in the Dinard Casino. The last I heard of him, he was still there, too busy at the tables to have any time for me."

Even while I was telling the guy that, I was trying to get the thing figured. They had tried to kidnap Barbie and now Barbie was dead. Had they shifted their sights and were now out to kidnap Elston? After all, there was an epidemic of it going. Snatch a fat cat and you collect a fat ransom. It had been done, and all too often the kidnapers had collected and gotten away with it. It was an answer of sorts, but only of sorts. What then had been the game with Barbie? Who would there have been to kick in with the ransom for her? Her Johnny? Nothing could be more obvious than that this would not be his way of playing the game. Erridge?

Okay. I drive a Porsche. I do all right, but I don't sit on any stack of millions. They could, of course, have been making a mistake. They could have thought Erridge was a lot fatter than he ever expects to be, but there was all that rifle fire at Les Andelys. They were going to bump Erridge off and grab the girl. It would have been one way of getting their hands on her, but they could hardly have expected to collect any ransom from a stiff.

I was telling myself that they were stupid. It was even possible that they were crazy, but this made no sense, not even some crazy kind of sense.

Yellow pants started toward me.

"It looks like I'm going to have to make you talk," he said.

He no more than got started. Mathilda was up and snarling. He stepped back.

Bandaged hand spoke up.

"Shoot the mutt," he said. "How much time are we going to waste?"

Yellow pants ignored him. He was talking only to me.

"Untie your feet," he said.

It was an order and a baffling one. It seemed to be a quick about-face. He had been on the point of getting rough, but Mathilda had changed his mind about that. Was he now going to have a try at winning me over with kindness?

So it was a gift horse. I worked at putting out of my mind all thoughts of Greeks and Trojans. I couldn't see how anything could come of it that wouldn't be an improvement in my situation. I was still going to be up against three guns; but, even if having my feet untied was going to do me no good, it would at least make me feel a shade less helpless.

Holding the gun on me, he watched from a safe distance while I carried out his order.

"That's right," he said when I had my legs freed. "Now stand up."

I stood.

"Pick the bitch up and hold her."

I took Mathilda up in my arms. She liked it there.

"Turn around."

I turned. I had no idea what it was for, but I couldn't read it as his having any notion of shooting me in the back. Keeping the .45 leveled at me, he circled us and went to the door. He threw it open and stepped away from it.

"Take her out to the hall," he said, "and shut the door on her. Don't try to get out there with her unless you think you need a slug in your knee."

I did as I was told. I was doing it with mixed feelings. I was losing my only ally, but then it was obvious that I would be losing her in any case. I preferred it this way. Shutting her out of the room was better than seeing them shoot her.

I had to be quick. Her feet had no more than touched the floor before she was whipping around and heading back in. I got the door shut before she could make it.

Yellow pants backed away to the window and perched on the sill. He never had his gun off me even for a second.

"Now we can talk without having her get in our way," he said.

She was scratching at the door and whining. Periodically she would break off for a moment or two of barking, but then she would be back at the scratching and whining.

"I know you haven't seen him," my questioner said. "Not that I'm taking your word for anything, but we have been keeping tabs on you. You couldn't have seen him without leading us to him, but you know where he is."

"Last I heard he was in Dinard," I said. "Otherwise . . ."

I shrugged.

"When was this "last" that you heard?"

"Morning two days ago. I had his secretary on the phone. He didn't say where Elston was, but there was nothing in what he did say to make me think Elston wasn't still in Dinard."

"He wasn't."

"Okay. Then you know more than I do. Why don't you try Elston's secretary? He's in touch."

"Very funny," he said.

"The best I can give you," I said.

There was a moment of silence. It seemed a strange silence, and then it came to me. I knew what I was missing. The scratching and whining had stopped, and this time it wasn't that Mathilda had taken time out to work in a spot of barking. There was no sound of any kind from the other side of the closed door.

I was remembering the road out of Guimiliau. She had left her mourning over the body to run out to the road to flag me down. Could she be doing it again? Was she running out of the house in an effort to find help and bring it back to me? It was a nice thought but a hopeless one. There was no place she could go, and no one would pick up her signals and follow her back to where I was.

I couldn't believe that she had just given up on me and gone off. I was picturing her out on the road. She would be there putting out useless signals. There would be no one who could catch her signals, nobody who would understand.

Then she came and it couldn't have been more sudden or more unexpected. It was as though she had appeared from nowhere. She came in the window. The first any of us knew she was there, she already had her teeth sunk into yellow butt's gun hand.

The gun dropped clattering to the floor. I jumped for it and I had it at the ready before the two startled lunkheads came out of their stupor enough to make the first move toward their shoulder holsters. Mathilda had the head man under control. I took care of the other two. Holding the gun on them, I gave them their orders. They couldn't have been more docile.

I had them pull out of their shoulder holsters, drop the holsters complete with guns on the floor, and kick the whole business over to me. Meanwhile yellow pants was flailing around, trying to beat Mathilda off, but she wasn't coming loose from his hand. He was yelling and he was cursing. Mathilda wasn't listening.

I called her off. She gave up on the hand and came to me. I herded the three of them together and kept them covered. Meanwhile I was thinking about the way Mathilda had come in that window. I had a vision of her flapping her ears and flying through the air, but I had to discard that. Her ears don't flap. They just dangle.

Now that the window was empty, almost immediately the doves came strutting to the sill, repossessing it. Seeing them, I tumbled to the obvious. They hadn't flown to settle on the sill. They had walked to it. That meant there was something out there they could walk on. Given that much hint, I could picture the ledge, an ornamental cornice that would run along just below window level.

When Matilda had given up on the door, she'd found an open hall window and through it she had heard our voices. That had done it. She'd nipped out the window, run along the ledge and had just zeroed in on what she was hearing.

We were in command, Mathilda and I, but I was wondering how long we might have. If this trio I had under the gun was the lot of them, we were all right, but there was nothing to say there wouldn't be more and that at any moment they wouldn't be coming through the door for another turning of the tables. I did what I could. I moved the three of them and stood them backed against the closed door. That way I had them covered and, if anyone opened the door behind them, he would be coming straight at my line of fire.

Yellow pants was holding his hand and whimpering.

"You going to let me bleed to death standing here?"

I didn't go in close to examine his bleeding hand. I could see all I needed from where I was. There was blood, but it wasn't spurting.

"You won't bleed to death," I said. "She didn't get an artery this time. I can also guarantee that you're all right for rabies. She's a healthy dog. Other infections? I don't know. She's had her teeth into some pretty cruddy flesh these last few days."

"We didn't hurt you any," he said. "We didn't do you any harm."

"You killed my girl."

"We were nowhere near your girl."

"That night at Mont St. Michel?"

"We didn't hurt her. You can't say we hurt her."

"Your dopes muffed that one. So your head man gave up on trusting them with anything. He took it on himself and he killed her."

"Mr. Elston? You out of your head?"

For that one I had a quick answer.

"Not me," I said. "You are."

It had suddenly come to me. I did know his way of speaking. I had heard it earlier only over the telephone, and a French telephone at that, through a lot of buzz and clatter. This was the secretary who had been keeping in touch, the guy who'd been insisting I keep him briefed on my itinerary just in case Elston all of a sudden might get around to wanting to bring Erridge to heel.

Once I'd caught that, of course, a lot of what had been bothering me came clear. That was how his two lugs had known we would be at Les Andelys. That they would find us at the Château Gaillard had been an easy guess for them. We were on a sightseeing tour, and in Les Andelys the Lion Heart's baby is the only thing to see. That was how they had known we were headed for Perros-Guirec to lie in wait for us there. They'd had to hurry because they hadn't had the word on the day's itinerary until he'd caught me at Vernon with that phone call just before Barbie and I had taken off. We'd made some stops en route, and I could guess that they hadn't. It explained their having been that bit ahead of us.

There was all the other stuff, though, that was still unexplained. How had they known about Guimiliau? It hadn't been on the itinerary I'd handed him. I hadn't known myself that we were going to hit the crazy calvary that afternoon. That had been an unplanned detour, made only on the spur of the moment and at Barbie's insistence. Nobody could have known about that unless they'd learned it from her. When I'd told the guy that his head man had killed her, I hadn't, of course, been thinking Elston. I'd been thinking her Johnny. I was still thinking her Johnny. So who was this guy? How did he get to be sitting on Elston's phone to take the calls I'd been trying to get to Elston?

Meanwhile he was looking at his hand.

"If I die of this," he said, "it'll be murder."

"You won't die of it," I told him. "You're going to talk, and the sooner you've told me what I need to know, the sooner you'll get to do something about your dog bite."

"Look," he said. "You're holding the guns. Okay. You've won. There's nothing more I can do. I tried every which way. So now all right. We'll pay."

The man was babbling.

"Shut up," I said, "and answer questions."

But he wasn't ready to shut up.

"You'll have to give us time to get the money," he said. "I can't reach down in my pants and just come up with it, not that kind of money. But you have my word. Tell Gibbs we're not fighting it any more. We've stayed away from the police and we'll go on staying away from them. We're going to pay. That's what you need to know, isn't it? Your car's downstairs in the driveway. I drove it over from Perros-Guirec myself. Take off and tell Gibbs. I'll get working on the money right away, right after I've had this hand fixed up."

"Okay," I said. "We can begin with that. Where's Gibbs?"

"Look. You've won. What more do you want? Do you have to go horsing around? We grabbed you. We were going to make you tell us where he is and where he's got Elston. If you had any sense, you'd tell us. You'd throw in with us. You'll not be standing good with Gibbs, you know, not now after you've knocked off his babe."

"Who the hell are you?" I asked.

"Oh, come off it, man. You know who I am."

"You're the guy I've been talking to on the telephone. You're the guy who's been pretending you're Elston's secretary."

"Pretending? How did you get me on the phone? It was on Elston's line, wasn't it? How would I be on Elston's line if I wasn't his secretary?"

"That's one of the things you're going to tell me and soon, unless you like standing there and bleeding."

"I'm Herb Graham," he said. "I wrote you to come to Dinard in the first place. You saw the signature on the letter: 'Herbert Graham for Alexander Elston.'"

I remembered the signature, but I wasn't taking it just on his say-so.

"You have ID?" I asked.

"In my wallet. In my back pocket. I can't get at it with this hand."

He was exaggerating. That hand wasn't so bad that it was useless. I guess he didn't want to get blood on those beautiful yellow slacks. I had one of the goons take the wallet out of that back pocket and pull the driver's license out of it for me to see. It said Herbert Graham and the picture matched. It went a long way toward explaining him and his pair of cohorts. They were amateurs at the kind of stuff they'd been trying to pull on me, rough enough but unknowing and unskilled.

"Okay," I said. "What did you want with the girl?"

"Trade her," Graham said. "Gibbs had Elston. If we had his girl, we could have made a trade. You spoiled that when you bumped her."

"Who the hell do you think I am?" I asked.

"I *know* who you are. You're Matthew Erridge."

"And?"

"And you've been working with Gibbs. He was going to kidnap Elston and he couldn't have his girl around when he did it. She'd be in the way and he couldn't leave her here in Dinard where we could get at her. So you took her off and you were supposed to be taking care of her for him. I don't know why you killed her. That'll be between you and Gibbs, but, if you are smart, you'll throw in with us. You're in trouble, man. You're in bad trouble. That Gibbs, he plays for keeps."

"I didn't kill her," I said.

"All right, but you were taking care of her and you let her get killed. You think that's going to make a big difference to Gibbs?"

"I guess we stand even," I said. "You've been thinking I

was working with Gibbs, and I've been thinking the same about you. You have me convinced. You weren't. Now you've got to believe me. I wasn't either."

I picked up the two holsters complete with the guns and I marched the three of them out of the room. I told them to lead the way to the nearest bathroom and I let Graham wash his dog bites, put some antiseptic on them, and bandage his hand. His goons helped with it. While they were busy with that, I did the talking. I finally had the whole thing straight in my head and I worked at putting them straight on it.

Everything had fallen into place and everything fitted. Barbie had worked on me to take her away because she had known what Gibbs had going and she hadn't wanted to be any part of it. I knew their record from what the gendarmes had told me. Their line had been burglary and armed robbery, and those are simple crimes. Kidnaping is something else, far more complicated. Barbie had been smart. She'd realized that Gibbs was moving out of their league. He was a professional thief and robber, but he was going to be an amateur kidnaper. She hadn't been about to have any of that. She walked out on him.

When the two fumblers had make the grab at her up at Mont St. Michel, she'd make the same mistake about them as I had. She'd thought they were working for Gibbs. She'd been so set on not going to the police because she'd been thinking just that. It could have been that even then she hadn't wanted to queer her Johnny's pitch, or it could merely have been that she had too much of a record with the police and was too much oriented to thinking of them as the enemy. Also, she would have been going to them with me. It could have been that she didn't want me learning about her record.

Then there had been Les Andelys and the Château Gaillard battlements and the try they'd made there at knocking me off. That had been too much for the kid. It had knocked her over. She was through with Gibbs, but she couldn't just leave it the way it was with Erridge a hunted man, a guy with a good chance of being dead on her account.

She'd called Gibbs and said she wanted to see him. He'd set it up for the meeting at Guimiliau. I was guessing that she'd had no intention of going back to him. She'd been thinking perhaps that she could make a trade. She'd tell him that they were through, and she'd tell him it wasn't because of me. It was because of him. Her trade would have been that she would keep clammed up and do nothing to spoil what he had going with Elston, and in exchange he was to leave her and me alone.

I could understand how it had worked out. Barbie had miscalculated. Her Johnny Gibbs wasn't the man to take anything like that lying down. He also wasn't the man who would trust anyone, much less a girl who had been his and who had left him for another man. It had been okay for a woman to know as much as she did about him as long as she was his woman and she was sharing his guilts. Once that was over, she was no longer any good to him. She had become a woman who knew too much. He couldn't let her go on living.

I told them all of that, and all the time I was talking I was seeing road maps in my head. I was also remembering things. They were things that hadn't meant much to me at the time, but now I was fitting them into my mental road maps and they were giving me something to think about. I wasn't handing Graham and his goons any of this stuff I was working out for myself. I had things to do and I didn't want them tagging after me and messing me up. I knew too much about the quality of their performance. Allies like those three I didn't need.

"So there's no way you can help us?" Graham said.

"There's one way," I said, "and I'll do it because I want to be all the help I can. I'll keep your guns. You guys will be better off without them. First thing you know, you'll be hurting yourselves with them."

They took that without a murmur. Maybe because they were recognizing how cockeyed stupid their every move had been. More likely it was because I wouldn't be leaving them unarmed. There would be more guns where these had come from. There were, after all, those rifles the two had been toting at Les Andelys. These guys probably had something like a full arsenal at their disposal.

I worked Graham for details of the kidnaping and for anything he might have been doing in an effort to deal with the situation—anything, that is, other than Operation Erridge. I knew all I needed to know about that effort.

The kidnaping evidently had been easy. Elston and Gibbs had been meeting day after day at the tables in the Casino. They had become buddy-buddy. The two goons had been working for Elston. He had taken them on as bodyguards, but Elston was a kind and considerate employer. His habit of staying at the tables till the last card was turned every night had been hard on his bodyguards. They were young. They needed their sleep.

So once Elston and Gibbs had become such great pals, Elston had stopped taking the bodyguards with him for his nights at the Casino. He didn't need them. He had his good, tough friend, Johnny Gibbs. It had become a routine. Gibbs would come by in his car to pick Elston up. They would go to the Casino together and, after their night of gambling, Gibbs would run Elston home and drop him off at this rented château.

They had been doing it that way for a few days. You'll remember that I'd seen them together at the Casino. The afternoon of the day I'd taken off with Barbie had begun no differently from the preceding days. That, however, was all that had been the same as before. That afternoon they never arrived at the Casino. Graham, however, hadn't known that till later. Nothing had come up all day that warranted disturbing the boss at his play. So the first he'd known that Elston was missing had been when the ransom call came through to him early in the morning.

"I knew it was Gibbs," he said. "I recognized his voice."

"Over the phone?" I asked.

"I knew the way he sounded over the phone," Graham explained. "I'd talked to him on the phone lots of times when he'd be calling Mr. Elston."

The call had been the standard garbage. Elston was safe. He hadn't been harmed. He was comfortable and, if everyone was sensible, he would come to no harm. How do you define "sensible"? Sensible is assembling a million bucks in cash, and sensible is keeping away from the police.

Sensible is breaking up the million five ways. It had to be two hundred thousand in dollars, and like amounts in sterling, French francs, Swiss francs, and Deutschemarks. Graham had taken careful note of the instructions and he'd promised to be sensible. He had explained, however, that the kidnaper would have to be sensible as well. He would have to be patient. He would have to understand.

"I told him I couldn't just reach down into my pants and come up with a million dollars just like that," Graham said. "I made a big deal about how it was going to take time to get the money, and more time to get it in the five different currencies."

"Can you get it?" I asked.

"I couldn't, not without Mr. Elston's authorization, but Gibbs took care of that. He made Mr. Elston write out an order on our New York office. That went to New York and the money has been transferred. It's in the bank here in Dinard and they're organizing the foreign exchange. It'll be ready tomorrow, and now we'll just have to pay it over. I've shot my bolt."

"Where do you pay it?"

"He telephones here every day at one o'clock. He set that up the first night when he called. I was to be at the phone ready to take his call at one in the afternoon every day. When I tell him the money is ready, he'll tell me where I'm to take it."

I looked at my watch.

"Then, he'll be calling within a half hour," I said.

"And I'll have to be downstairs to pick up the phone," Graham said.

I herded them out of the bathroom.

"Okay," I said. "Where's the phone?"

"Can I go down?"

I knew that there would be at least one extension. I'd had phone calls from Elston and they had been the standard big-shot routine. Secretary gets you on the phone. Mr. Big wants to talk to you, but you're kept waiting till Mr. Big comes on. Once he starts talking, you hear the click. That's the secretary hanging up his phone.

We went downstairs to wait for the call. That is, Graham and Mathilda and I went down. I locked the pair of bodyguards in that attic room where they had taken me. I wasn't ready to put anything like complete trust in these guys. If I was going to be juggling a telephone and a gun at the same time, one man to keep covered was going to be enough.

I filled Graham in on how we were going to play it. When the phone rang, we were going to be ready on the two extensions and we were going to pick up simultaneously. That was going to be easy. The phones were in adjoining rooms, but one was on a long cord. It could be carried through the door between the rooms. Graham was going to do all the talking. I would only be listening, and Graham was to give no indication that he wasn't alone.

"What are you going to tell him?" I asked.

"I'll have to tell him that the money is here and it'll be ready tomorrow."

"And when he tells you where you're to deliver it, are you going to tip the police off to the pickup place?"

"And get Mr. Elston killed?"

I couldn't tell him there wasn't a good chance of that. After all, Johnny Gibbs was a killer. He'd murdered Barbie. Also, the way he was playing this kidnaping, it seemed to me that he would have to kill Elston. How could he leave the man alive to identify him? Graham, of course, could tell the police that he'd recognized Gibbs on the telephone; but how well would such identification stand up in a court. Gibbs had killed Barbie. What was going to stop him from making it two? Anyhow, it was Elston's million bucks, and I owed Elston nothing. The way I was seeing it, Graham could sweat the kidnaping out. I had a score of my own to settle with Johnny Gibbs.

"I'm going to be there," I said.

"What if he says I must come alone?" Graham asked.

"You'll go alone, but I'll be there."

"And you'll get Mr. Elston killed."

"Like I got the girl killed? That was different."

He opened his mouth to make some further protest, but the phone rang and he swallowed whatever it was that he had been about to say. Our simultaneous pickup on the two phones went perfectly. I gave him the signal and he performed. I had the gun on him and I had Mathilda lying at my feet. With all that going for me, this Graham guy wasn't the man to make any tries at crossing me up.

It was Gibbs calling and right on schedule, but, apart

from the precise timing, there was nothing about this call that ran to the form Graham had described to me. The way Graham had told it, Gibbs would come on and ask for a progress report on the preparation of the ransom payment. He would put Elston on to say he was in good shape and was being well treated. Then Gibbs would repeat his warnings against trying any tricks and, setting up the next call for one o'clock the next day, he would hang up.

His choice of the time for making these calls was understandable. One hour after noon is smack in the middle of every Frenchman's lunch hour. You have a whole country tying on the feedbag, and there's no country anywhere where lunch is taken more seriously than in France. Everybody's busy with knife and fork. Everybody has his eyes glued to his plate. It's the perfect time for secret movements and secret acts. Nobody's going to be eavesdropping. Nobody's going to hear.

Gibbs came on, but this time he came on rough. Graham had been stalling him. Graham had been playing games. Now the games were finished. Gibbs was through waiting. Graham could pay the ranson and he'd have Elston alive and unharmed.

"No more Mr. Nice Guy," Gibbs said. "You stall me some more and Elston's going to get hurt. He's going to get hurt so bad that he'll wish he was dead. You try one more trick and Elston'll get that wish. You'll be getting him back, but not for anything but to plant him."

Graham tried to protest. He went into his routine about how it took time to get the money and more time to work out all that exchange. Gibbs was having none of that. He broke in.

"In case you haven't heard," Gibbs said, "the babe you were working on is gone. She got iced last night. Even if you'd nabbed her, it wouldn't have done you any good. You think you know who I am. That's why you were after her, but you were never right about that. Anyhow, she's gone, so get it through your head now. There's no way in the world you can get at me. I'm holding all the cards and you're going to pay. It's today or else."

That attempt to pretend that he wasn't Johnny Gibbs was feeble, but the very fact that he was trying it was saying something. Ransom or no ransom, he wasn't going to be able to let Elston stay alive. The way he was running this kidnaping, he was going to have to kill his man.

"It can't be today," Graham said.

"That's what you've been saying every day. You've had plenty of time. Today."

"But the money isn't ready. I swear to you."

"You better talk to Elston," Gibbs said. "Hold on."

Elston came on and he also came on rough. Part of what he said was pleading, but more of it was anger and threat. Graham was playing with his life, and who had ever authorized Graham to do that?

"It's *my* money," Elston told him. "I ordered payment. So what are you trying to do? Get me killed? Get me crippled?"

"But, Mr. Elston, I thought . . ."

Elston didn't want to hear what Graham thought. He broke in on him.

"Don't *but* me. You're not paid to think. You're paid to follow orders. You had my orders. If I'm going to have the least bit of a hard time before I'm out of this, I'll hold you responsible. You're the one who's going to be wishing he was dead."

"But, Mr. Elston, I can't."

"What do you mean you can't?"

"The money isn't ready."

Elston exploded.

"Isn't ready?" he screamed. "What have you been doing all this time? What beside all that crazy business with some girl?"

"I've been getting the money." Graham was sweating. "It's here. It's in the bank, but all that exchange he wants. That won't be ready till tomorrow. I'm going to pay it. I'll do exactly as he says, but tomorrow. The bank's working on the exchange. They'll have it by tomorrow noon."

Elston turned away from the phone. I could tell by the change in the sound of his voice. He was talking to Gibbs, passing on to him the word about the exchange.

Gibbs came back on.

"Okay," he said. "This is your last chance. You can forget about the exchange. You say it's in the bank. What's it in? Dollars?"

"That's right," Graham said. "It's in dollars."

"I'll take it in dollars then, dollars and as much in the other currencies as they have on hand. They always have some on hand. The full million any way it comes, but today. You're paying it over today."

I was listening to all of this and, as it went on and on, I was thinking about how easy the thing could have been if Graham had only gone to the police. The way the call was stretching out, there would have been more than enough time for pinpointing the spot from which Gibbs was talking. There would easily have been enough time for the police to have closed in on the place and, since Gibbs had Elston at the phone with him, they would have been a cinch for grabbing Gibbs and freeing Elston.

I had begun to wonder about Gibbs. All right—the man was a pro, but not at kidnaping. Still, it seemed impossible that he wouldn't have known that, for a man in his spot, phone calls had to be quick and they had to be kept brief. Even an amateur would know that calls can be traced. All it takes is for the telephone people to be given sufficient time.

It had to be that Gibbs was that sure of Graham. Even after Barbie had told him about Mont St. Michel and Les Andelys and he'd had it figured that Graham hadn't been playing it straight with him, he was still that sure of Graham. It occurred to me that, if anything, he would now be even more sure of the man. Graham had made his try and Graham had failed. Gibbs was confident that he now had Graham eating out of his hand. From where I was standing, where I could see the sweating secretary as well as hear him, I was in a position to know just how right Gibbs was about the guy. Graham was licked every which way. Gibbs did have him eating out of his hand.

Gibbs snapped out his orders and Graham listened. The drop was to be made that evening at seven o'clock. It was to be seven on the dot, no earlier and no later. Graham was to take the road south to Dinan and then west through Lamballe and Morlaix, on through St. Thégonnec and Kermat. Just beyond Kermat he would take a left turn on D. 31.

Hearing that much, I held my breath. I knew what was coming and I couldn't believe it.

IX.

I had to believe it. The instructions were detailed and explicit. At seven precisely, Graham was to be at Guimiliau. He was to go into the parish close. He couldn't miss it. It was the only thing there was in Guimiliau. He'd know a churchyard when he saw one, and he'd know the calvary. It was the biggest hunk of sculpture in the place.

Gibbs was better than a guidebook. He had the mouth of hell pinpointed, and he told Graham exactly where he would find it. Graham was to tuck the money into the mouth of hell and he was to take off without looking back. That would be all.

"If someone else comes along and grabs the money before you pick it up," Graham argued, "you'll think I didn't leave it."

Graham was looking at me.

"No one will come along," Gibbs said. "You wait there in the churchyard till a car comes through on the road. The driver will toot his horn five times as he goes by. You listen and count them. When you hear the five toots, you put the money where I told you, run straight to your car, and take off—and not in the direction the car went. You don't follow it. You go the other way and you don't look back."

Graham spluttered.

"Mr. Elston . . ." he began.

"When you get back to Dinard, you'll wait for a call. It

may be the usual time tomorrow or it may be earlier. Either way, it will be Elston. He'll tell you where to go to pick him up."

"I can't do that," Graham wailed. "How do I know?"

Gibbs cut in on him.

"You don't know," he said. "You just have to trust me. I've been playing straight with you, and you're the one who's been playing games. So, if it's you trust me or I trust you, who takes the risks? Not me, brother."

"But . . ."

"You want it from Elston?" Gibbs asked.

Without waiting for an answer he put Elston on, and that was as before. Graham wasn't to do any thinking. Graham wasn't to have any ideas of his own. Graham was to take his orders and follow them to the letter.

"You've come too close to getting me killed," Elston said. "Now you're going to quit all that and behave yourself."

"Yes, Mr. Elston. If you want it that way, Mr. Elston."

"I want it that way," Elston said. "I want to go on living."

Gibbs came back on but only to hang up. Graham turned to me.

"You heard him," he said. "You'll be my witness."

"I'll be your witness."

"You heard what they said. You can't go with me."

"I heard what they said. *You* take Elston's orders. *I* don't."

"You'll get him killed."

"I'll try not to, but that's not my problem or yours. It's Elston's. Pay or not pay, in the plan Elston's not going to live. He can identify Gibbs, and not just on a telephone voice."

"He doesn't think so. You heard him. I have to follow orders."

"That's right," I said. "Elston's orders, Gibbs's orders, and my orders. You have no choice. I have you under the gun."

He thought I had a plan of action, and I wasn't about to disillusion him. All I knew was that nobody was going to deal Erridge out, not at this stage of the game, not after Barbie. What I was going to do depended on how things shaped up. I was going to be there and I was going to do what I could. That was all I knew.

He wanted to take off for the bank, but I wasn't quite ready to go, and I wasn't letting him out of my sight. I made him give me the keys to the Porsche. Then I took him back upstairs and locked him away with the other two. I went out to Baby and pulled a bag out of her trunk. Back there in Perros-Guirec I hadn't bothered to unload her or to unpack. I had a bad moment when I went into the car trunk. Barbie's bags were still in there, not that I needed anything to remind me.

Inside the château it didn't take much exploring to find Elston's room. It had the regal look, but it also had specific stuff like silver-backed hairbrushes with his monogram on them. That château was a big place, and it all looked clean and well-kept. I wondered about servants, but it was a good bet that they weren't going to be around for a while. It was a cinch that Graham had gotten rid of them at least for the day. With the plans he'd had for me, he wouldn't have wanted them hanging around.

I shaved and showered in Elston's bathroom and I changed my clothes. Mathilda was staying close to me all the time, and it occurred to me that it was a long time since either she or I had last eaten. I found the kitchen and checked the larder. There was an enormous refrigerator and it was well stocked. I pulled out a filet mignon and gave it to Mathilda. There was no dog dish, so she had to take it off a Sèvres plate, and a Sèvres bowl did her all right for a water dish. I made do with a hunk of bread, butter, and foie gras. I wasn't taking the time to look for the wine cellar, but there were some bottles chilling in the refrigerator. They were all sauternes, and that figured. Elston and company would go for sweet wines. I tapped a bottle of Barsac —not exactly to my taste, but the best of what was ready to hand.

Don't think I wasn't giving a thought to my prisoners up in the attic, but if they'd gone without breakfast, that would have been nobody's fault but their own. They could wait.

Having taken our snack, we went upstairs and brought Graham down. The two goons wanted out. Graham had filled them in on Elston's orders and they were promising to be good. I wasn't listening. I was past trusting anyone, and that pair least of all.

Graham drove us to the bank. I had his gun, but I was carrying it in one of the shoulder holsters I'd taken from the goons. I didn't have to make any display of it in public. I had Mathilda, and she was more than enough to guarantee his good behavior.

Even in the most compactly done-up bundle, the money bulked large. From what I remembered of the calvary's mouth of hell, the package was never going to tuck into the hole, but that could be Graham's worry. He was going to have to leave it on the ground below the hell mouth. I didn't think Gibbs was going to mind stooping to pick it up. I did, however, have the thought that it could be a good time for taking him, when he was stooping down with his hands full of that big bundle.

I was hoping he would have Elston with him for the

pickup. That would make the thing easy. If he was playing a lone hand, it wouldn't matter too much. All I had to do was take him. If, by the time I was through with him, he was still not ready to tell me where he had Elston tucked away, the police could take over and sweat it out of him.

I didn't want to think about the possibility that he wasn't playing a lone hand. There was that outside chance that he would be leaving Elston in the hands of a helper and that the instructions might be to kill Elston and take off if Gibbs didn't return from the pickup, but I knew what the gendarmes had told me about the Interpol information on Johnny Gibbs. He had always worked alone until he had joined up with Barbie. I just couldn't believe that in the few days since Barbie had walked out on him and taken off with me, he had found himself another girl, one he could trust and one with a stronger stomach for violence than Barbie had shown.

There were going to be risks, of course, since the one thing I knew for sure about the man was that he was a killer, but it seemed to me that once I had him and I'd turned him over to the flics, he would be eager to make whatever deal he could this side of the guillotine.

Back at the château we had lunch and we fed the goons. I didn't lock them up again. It wasn't necessary, since I was going away from there, but I didn't give them back their guns. I kept one gun on me and packed the others away in the Porsche's trunk. I would have liked to give one to Mathilda, but it could have been no good to her. That pup has everything, but she doesn't have a trigger finger.

We made an early start out of Dinard. Graham was nervous. He had an itch to get going. For a moment or two when we first were taking off, he cheered up a bit. I let him pull out, and Mathilda and I didn't get in the car with him, as we had on the trip to the bank. He grinned thinking I had changed my mind about coming along, but we piled into the Porsche and rolled out to the road on his tail.

I'm not going to say he didn't try to get away from us and don't think he didn't have good wheels, but his were out of the Elston stable. That means he was driving a heap that had been built to impress. Baby, on the other hand, is built for speed and handling even though she is pretty to look at. He soon learned that it was no good trying to outrun her.

I had the car radio on and I was keeping an ear out for the news. I thought they might still be talking about Barbie. I was even thinking there might be something about that American, Matthew Erridge, who had been mixed up with the murdered woman and who had now skipped out on his hotel bill at Perros-Guirec. There was nothing of that, and I took to wondering whether Graham had gone through the formalities of checking me out and paying the bill before he had driven Baby out of there. It was something I was going to have to ask him.

If there was anything happening anywhere in the world apart from the Breton farmers' strike, those Breton newscasters were not interested. At first I thought they were still talking about those cabbage barricades I'd tangled with on the roads around St. Brieuc, but the place names were wrong.

They were talking about a new blockage, more action on the highways. I heard Quimper, Pontivy, Châteaulin, and Carhaix-Plouguer. The northern highway complex had been hit first, and now the farmers were striking to the south, tying up roads through the interior and out to the west coast. From the reports I gathered that nothing had changed but the locale. Otherwise the picture was the same —the great truckloads of cabbages dumped on the highways, the great green mounds manned by the embattled farmers, the shotguns and the ax handles and the pitchforks.

I could understand why the newsmen had thought for nothing else. This was, after all, France, and cabbages are food. There's nothing like a barricade to catch a Frenchman's attention, and nothing like food to rivet it.

It was not yet six o'clock when we hit the last town before Guimilaiu. It was the town I'd gone to after finding Barbie's body, and, as far as I'd come up with any kind of plan, this town was a part of it. I pulled around in front of Graham's car and waved him to a stop. We parked in front of the little zinc, and I climbed out and went to talk to Graham.

"This isn't it," he said. "It's the next place down the road."

"I know where it is," I said. "We're early. I'll buy you a drink."

He wanted one. It showed all over him.

"I don't know that I should," he said.

"All you've got to do is drop a package, and you can do that drunk or sober. Anyhow, I'm not going to get you drunk. I'll just buy you a drink."

He needed no more persuading. He had his bundle locked in the trunk of his car. He was nervous about it. Even walking the few steps into the café, he went with his head turned, never taking his eyes off the car. His eyes, of course, weren't the only ones on it. If Baby alone had caused a sensation among the patrons of that bar, now it was Baby in the richest of company.

My friend the pompier came out from behind the bar to embrace me. Since Graham was with me, he embraced Graham as well. We ended up with more drink than I'd promised, since, after I'd bought, we had to have one on the house. It was an event. In France they don't often come on the house.

I had come to the café to ask a small favor. Over the drinks the atmosphere was right. I wanted to leave the Porsche for a while. Could I leave it in the care of my bartending fireman buddy? There was no problem. He was mine to command, and this was only a small thing I was asking. I was to have no worries. He would keep Baby safe. His eyes would never come off her. He reached down behind the bar and came up with a bung starter.

"If anybody so much as touches your beautiful automobile," he said.

Flourishing his weapon, he walked with us out to the cars. The little crowd that had gathered dropped back a few paces. Fixing them with a menacing glare, he snapped out his orders. The whole gang rallied to the cause. There wouldn't be a man in the village who would not be mounting guard over Baby. I was leaving her in good hands.

For a moment or two back at the bar Graham had relaxed a bit. Now he was more jumpy than ever.

"What are you going to do?" he asked.

"We're going with you," I said. "Mathilda and I. When he drives by to give you the signal, we don't want him seeing two cars. That'd be a dead giveaway."

"And you and the mutt won't be?"

"Mathilda and I will be out of sight. He'll see nothing but the one car and you."

"And if you can't keep her quiet?"

"She'll be quiet. She graduated from obedience school top of her class—*magna cum laude, Phi Beta Kappa*. You should be so smart."

He didn't like it, but he had no choice. I hadn't unholstered my gun, but he knew I had it where I could reach it, and there was also Mathilda, who had her teeth even more at the ready. For the moment, furthermore, I was among friends. I was standing shoulder to shoulder with my buddy and his bung starter. We were surrounded by his cohorts.

"I've got to hope you're right," Graham sighed.

He climbed in behind the wheel. I went into the back seat and took Mathilda with me. I waited till we had rolled out of the little town and had gone around a bend in the road. The boys back at the zinc were my buddies, but it was no good giving them too much to think about. As soon as we were out of their sight, I slid down to the floor of the car and curled up cozily with Mathilda close beside me.

That way we rode into Guimiliau. Graham parked the way I told him to, at the side of the road, close up against the roadside shrubbery. Without rising up to where anyone could see us, Mathilda and I slipped out of the car and took cover in the bushes. Graham looked at his watch. I looked at mine. It was just ten minutes of seven. The old lady who had been such a slow study with the arithmetic involved in five postcards at twenty centimes each, came out of her shop and took a long look at Graham and the car.

Dressed as he was and driving that luxurious monster of an automobile, in the eyes of any shopkeeper he had to look like a potential customer, a late-arriving tourist who would be good for the sale of at least a franc's worth of postcards, if not some souvenirs like a pottery copy of the mouth of hell done as an ashtray.

I was watching her from the bushes. After looking him over, she behaved as though the potential customer wasn't there. Moving with a speed and efficiency that couldn't have been more at odds with the pace she had shown me on my one encounter with her, she locked her shop door, slapped the shutters up over door and shop window, mounted a bicycle, and went pedaling off at a clip that could have stood her in good stead in any bike race.

When she was gone, there was still a full minute to go before the dot of seven. The timing was too neat. Now I had another thing to think about. It hadn't been just a break of the luck for Gibbs when this old dame had held me up in her shop with her slow-paced arithmetic. The whole thing had been prearranged. Gibbs had left nothing to chance. I wondered how much it had cost him to buy those delaying tactics.

I put the thought aside for later consideration. Graham was out of the car and around to the trunk. He took out the money package and, returning to his place behind the wheel, put it on the seat beside him. Time clicked to seven and went clicking on past. I drew the revolver and checked it. It was as ready as I was. I returned it to the holster. I wasn't going to use it until after I had taken him. Jumping him from behind when he was stooped down and had his hands full of the big parcel, I should have it easy. I wasn't going to need a gun for that part of it.

The gun was going to be for bringing him in. Following instructions, Graham and the car were going to be off and gone before Gibbs would be back to pick up the money. So Mathilda and I were going to be there with our prisoner and no transport except for his wheels. We were going to have to take him back to where we'd left Baby and where I could get word to the gendarmes. I knew the distance. It was just over three kilometers. They would have to be done at gunpoint.

With Mathilda close at my heels I came out of the bushes and dashed across the road into the parish close. We had a choice of tombstones, but there was one that was the easy winner. It was close to the calvary, no more than four feet away. It was on the side that had the mouth of hell and it was a big one, more than tall enough and more than broad enough to give the pup and me ample cover and concealment.

Tucked in back there, we waited for the passing car and the five toots of the horn. The sun was slipping toward the horizon. You know how it seems to pick up speed as it pulls close to its setting. The lengthening shadows marched across the churchyard. The lowering sun dropped down behind the calvary, and the shadow of it crept over us. I kept looking at my watch. Gibbs was late. It was twenty after seven when the shadow reached us. I didn't mind. Time was on our side. No chance now that when I had to move in and take him, I could be blinded by sunset glare.

Graham was having the twitches. Taking his parcel with him, he got out of the car and trotted to where he could look around the bend of the road. Evidently he could see nothing coming from that direction. He reversed and trotted to the bend we had taken coming into Guimiliau. He could see nothing around that bend either. He returned to the car and waited some more. Even seated behind the wheel, he was in constant motion, raising his arm to look at his watch, turning his head to see if there was a car coming up behind him, leaning forward to the windshield to peer at the road ahead of him, as though coming that few inches closer could bring into sight a car that he wouldn't have seen if he were sitting back.

He sweated it out till ten of eight. Then, after having again trotted back and forth to reconnoiter in both directions, he came into the parish close to talk to me.

"It's almost eight o'clock," he said. "He isn't coming. Somehow he knows you're here. You've wrecked it. I knew you would. Mr. Elston . . ."

"Cool it," I said. "Keep your pants on. So he's late. No need for him to be on time. He knows he can keep you waiting. He knows he has you where he wants you. He'll come when he's good and ready, or he won't come. He maybe set this up as a test run, just making sure that you'll follow orders and come alone."

"And he'll know that I didn't come alone."

"How will he know that?"

"If he doesn't show up himself, how will he know that I came at all?"

"The old woman. She waited till you'd showed. Then she put up her shutters quick and took off."

Graham blinked and swallowed hard.

"He had her watching?"

"Could be. He had her holding me up in her shop while he was taking off with the girl. This is just another little chore he could be having her do."

"Then she told him you were here. That's why he hasn't come. I knew it was no good."

"She didn't see me."

"How do you know she didn't?"

"She was nowhere where she could have seen me. She doesn't have X-ray eyes. She saw you and she saw the car. She took a good look, but she didn't see me."

"I wish I could be sure of that," Graham moaned. "Mr. Elston . . ."

He kept saying "Mr. Elston" and fading out with the rest of it unfinished. Maybe he was thinking that Elston was going to be dead or maybe he was just thinking of himself, that Elston would be having his hide for messing things up. Whichever, it was a thought he couldn't bear to put into words.

I was waiting, thinking that this time he might finish it,

but then I couldn't wait. I had Mathilda under my hand, and I felt the tremor in her that would be the beginning of a bark. I stroked her and whispered to her.

"No, Matty, no."

Then I heard it and I turned quickly to Graham.

"Get away from me," I said. "Car coming."

He jumped away and then, thinking better of it, he slowed down and strolled back toward the road. The sound Mathilda had picked up was growing rapidly in volume. A car came around the bend before Graham had made it out of the churchyard.

It didn't go rolling on through and it didn't sound its horn, even the first toot. It pulled up. At first sight of it, I was amazed that Gibbs should be doing himself so well. The car came close to being an identical twin to the Elston wheels Graham had out on the road. Then I remembered that Gibbs had been picking Elston up and driving him to the Casino. I started to tell myself that it could have been that for such a purpose Gibbs had needed a car this rich. Perhaps the great Elston couldn't have been seduced into anything less.

Graham was ahead of me in recognizing it, and why not? I was seeing the car for the first time. Graham knew it well. Also, he was out in the open where he could get a better look at its occupants. I was behind the tombstone working at not being seen.

Then they were talking and I knew the voices. It began with Graham giving them hell.

"What are you doing here? You're ruining everything. He should have left you locked up."

"We had to come."

"What do you mean you had to come? Who told you to come? Who told you to mix in?"

"*He* did. *Him,* he's got Elston. He telephoned and told us to go tell you."

Graham simmered down and I came out from behind my tombstone and walked over to join the conference.

"Tell me what?" Graham was asking.

He sounded desperate. If he'd ever had any faith in these two goons of his, that was long gone. Now he was doubting that they could be capable of taking even a simple message and transmitting it correctly.

"He said to tell you he wouldn't be coming today. He was held up and he couldn't make it. He said you should go home and wait for him to call you. He said you should keep the dough handy because he's going to be calling you."

"Did he put Mr. Elston on? Did Mr. Elston tell you anything?"

"He didn't put Mr. Elston on. He was somewhere he didn't have Mr. Elston with him."

"How do you know that?" This was a question I asked.

"We asked to talk to Mr. Elston. He said we couldn't. He said Mr. Elston was all right, but Mr. Elston wasn't there. He said there was nothing wrong. He was just held up and he couldn't make it tonight. That's all."

Graham groaned.

"Now he's playing games," he said. "He's going to raise the ante."

"Let Elston worry about that," I said. "I need a lift back to my car."

"They'll take you," Graham said.

"Where are you going?"

"Back to Dinard as fast as I can. I've got to be there for when he calls."

"That's right," I said. "You be there."

His two bully boys weren't happy about it. They didn't like riding with Mathilda and me at their backs. Both of us made them nervous, but Mathilda more than me. Everything had come together for me. I was busy with the road maps I was reading in my mind.

I was remembering Barbie. She had wanted to go everywhere and see everything, but it had been a peculiarly limited everything. There had been the one exception: Quiberon, the Carnac area. I'd said no more than Quiberon and she had picked up on it immediately. She had known the neighborhood. She had known it was near Carnac, and she had known what Carnac is like. She'd gone right into it. She didn't want to see the menhirs and the dolmens. Druids gave her the creeps. She didn't want to go anywhere near them. Nothing else gave her the creeps, not dungeons and not that hysterically gruesome calvary. When I'd suggested the beach at Quiberon, her rejection of it had been almost frenzied. Everything else I'd suggested she'd jumped at, but not that one place. We couldn't go anywhere near it.

I was building the road pattern in my mind. The farmers had struck again, and this time the cabbage heads were rolling on the highways to the south of where we were. Gibbs had called and he couldn't put Elston on. He had called from somewhere along the road. It had to be that he'd made that call from the far side of a cabbage barricade.

X.

Back at the café we were a sensation. Every time I turned up there, it was with yet another superheap. I was establishing myself as a guy with an unending supply of the most expensive wheels. Every eye in the village was popping.

I told the goons to drop me at the café and to take off.

"Maybe Graham needs you," I said. "I don't."

They asked no questions. They couldn't have been happier. Having Mathilda and me off their backs was like a new lease on life. They took off and they were gone before my bartender pal had finished pouring the three drinks he'd begun setting up at the sight of us. I told him it didn't matter. He could keep pouring. It was going to be drinks for everybody and on me. Nobody was surprised. Here at last was an American who acted like an American. They'd seen it often enough in the Westerns every Frenchman loves. So isn't it the American way?

It was like my first time there. All the talk was about the farmers' strike and the barricaded highways. As before, they were in two camps, those who deplored it and those who applauded; but either way, they knew where the action was. I had picked up from the news reports the outlines of the road picture. Now they filled in those outlines for me.

It was the central tier of highways that had been hit this time. The strikers had blocked the coastal highway south from Brest, and the west-east run between Quimper and Rennes. The radio had fed me that much, but my drinking buddies were filling me in on the exact points where the barricades had been set up. They were giving me everything I needed to know, and I had to hope that their information was solid. It was verifying all my hunches on why Gibbs hadn't been able to get through to Guimiliau. If he had taken the shortest route up from Carnac, he would have made it more than halfway, only to be blocked at Carhaix-Plouguer. To move eastward from there to any roads that were open, he would have had to go all the way back to Carnac and start all over again.

I went out to Baby and came back with a road map. We spread it over the bar and I traced the route I had in mind. No good. It was blocked here, here, and here. I had been hoping that the barricades might have been less well placed and that a couple of short jogs to the east or west could have taken me around them, but where they were spotting them, I was licked. The only route I could work out from the map was going to take me on a wide swing to the east, clear out of Brittany, and then south by the Normandy roads till I could cut back west and come to the coast miles to the south of where I wanted to be. It was possible, but it was going to mean driving all night and well into the next day.

We kicked it around and they came up with the little roads the map didn't show, roads the farmers knew, the ones they were using to get around their own barricades. They zigged and they zagged. Baby wouldn't make the time on them she could make on the highways, but they would get me to Carnac in half the time I would have needed for the broad eastward swing I'd worked out from the map.

They were all for my staying over until morning. They

were certain I would get lost if I tried to do their route in the dark. After a good night's drinking, I could do it by daylight, and for a man with a skinful of calvados all that zigging and zagging they'd laid out might come naturally.

I had to beg off. I had to explain that I had urgent business down Carnac way and I couldn't wait for morning. I promised to be back after I'd finished my business. We would have our night of drinking then.

There was nothing wrong with the café grapevine. Those babies knew their roads, and they had the exact knowledge for pinpointing the spots where the action was. It was a long night's driving, but we did all right. We worked that road web without once going astray. Dawn caught up with us while we were skirting Vannes, and we were only just outside Carnac when the sun broke the horizon. When you are just outside Carnac, you'll be going past the alignments—great stretches of open country where the menhirs stand in ordered rows. It's an impressive sight anytime of day, but at sunrise it's something to set the hairs at the back of a man's neck to prickling.

The ancient stones seem to catch fire from the touch of the sun. Their long, daybreak shadows stripe the ground. It is a stage setting for the magical. In such a place and at such a moment a man can surprise himself. He gets sucked into looking for miracles, and it wasn't only that I was thinking that I needed one.

I had been carrying on through the night, riding a big high. Everything had clicked. Everything was working for me. All the evidence had been adding up. All the logic had been right. Two and two had been making four, and I was headed straight for Gibbs and his kidnap hideaway. So there I was, but I had come as far as the signs could take me. I wasn't beginning to doubt the signs. They were all right; but, riding on them I had come as far as I could hope to go. They had taken me to this Carnac area, but now what? Would it be in the town? Along the plage? Down the peninsular road to Quiberon? Somewhere along the Côte Sauvage?

I had run out of indicators. The possibilities were too many and too widespread. I was in the right stretch of country. I never had the first moment's doubt of that, but now where was I to look? I had far too much country on my hands. You are probably wondering how I could have come this far without having thought of the problem before.

I had thought of it. I had known that I was going to come up against it, but I had been thinking I was going to have something working for me. There had been those phone calls and always at one o'clock, neatly in the middle of the inviolable French lunchtime. There had been two things about those calls—their timing, and the fact that Gibbs had always had his captive with him when he was making them.

I had been assuming that the calls hadn't been made from any telephone in the hideaway. It would have been the most elementary precaution to make the calls from a public telephone or, better still, from an assortment of public telephones. Now, if a kidnaper is going to take his captive out in public so that the captive can talk over a public phone, the kidnaper has a problem. He's exposing himself to serious risks. How does he go about minimizing those risks? In France he chooses a time for his calls when nobody would be likely to eavesdrop on him, that time of day when everyone is seriously involved with the midday meal.

I knew where a man would have to go to find a public telephone. There aren't telephone booths sprinkled all over the place in the Carnac area. He had been using the phone at the end of the bar in one café or another. I'd been planning on making a round of the cafés, asking about two Americans who kept very much to themselves and who always stayed very close together. The most peculiar thing about these two Americans, however, was that they chose lunchtime to make long-distance telephone calls. I was counting on the good Breton barman to have taken notice of that. I had been hoping that even for Americans it would be considered a memorable case of misplaced priorities.

I know this sounds as though I was trying to have it both ways, figuring that the one o'clock time had been chosen because during his lunchtime no Frenchman would take notice of anyone's peculiar behavior, and now figuring the exact opposite—that notice would have been taken of the strange timing of a long-distance call.

It was only a seeming contradiction, however, because there was no French barman who, under the circumstances, would not both take notice and pay no attention. I'll have to explain that. When I talk about the public telephone at the end of the bar, it is just an ordinary instrument. It has no coin slots. You make your call, the operator comes on and tells you what the charges are, and you pay the money to the barman.

Choosing that one o'clock time for the calls, Gibbs had set it up so that he could talk and he could put Elston on to talk, with no worry that there might be anyone hovering nearby to overhear any part of the conversation. That a barman would be likely to find a long distance call made at that hour more memorable than one made at another time of day, Gibbs would have considered relatively unimportant. The important consideration would have been that no one should have any inkling of the content of those calls.

I had known all along that a tour of cafés to ask about two such strange Americans would be grabbing at straws, but I'd been telling myself that there might well be straws to grab at.

In the light of the rising sun, however, as I drove past those mysterious rows of prehistoric stones, I ran into a procession. It filled the road. I was forced to stop and wait while the celebrants streamed past the car to turn off the road into the field of menhirs.

They were barefoot. They were young. They were uniformly bearded and uniformly dressed in grubby white robes of some coarse, homespun stuff. They weren't hooded and, as they streamed past me, they kept chattering. It was all English chatter and it was in unmistakably American English. As they came off the road, row after row of them, they flung themselves flat on the ground in the direction of the rising sun and, lining themselves up neatly along the stripes of sunlight between the long menhir shadows, crawled on their bellies toward the sunrise.

I had run into an infestation of latter-day Druids, and American ones at that. No American can travel so far that he won't find that there are crazies among his countrymen who have traveled even farther. I'm accustomed to that. I've long since learned to take them in stride, but that one day in that one place I didn't need them. What was this going to do for my inquiries about a pair of Americans who had been behaving oddly? These Druids were dampening.

The last of them surged past and, turning off the road, dropped to their bellies. Mathilda and I left them to their devotions and drove on into the town. It was shuttered and sleeping. Nothing seemed to be stirring anywhere. We moved on to Carnac Plage. I parked there and took Mathilda for a run on the beach. We were both in need of the stretch after our long night of driving. I was trying to cling to some last shreds of hope that I might be able to manage something, but it was going to be at least a couple of hours before I could even try. I had to wait till people were up and about.

We had the beach completely to ourselves, Mathilda and I, and I was remembering a morning when we'd had the Dinard beach all to ourselves. It had been the three of us then and we'd gone swimming.

I don't know if it was for memory's sake or in the hope of clearing my head. I skinned out of my clothes and hit the water. Mathilda didn't come after me. She stayed back on the beach standing guard over my stuff. It was only a quick swim. Even though that early-morning water was brutally cold, it didn't clear my head. It came to me that I'd been one full night and most of another without sleep. My eyes had been open too long. The lids had grown so heavy that I felt I was muscling them open.

I came out of the water and used my T-shirt to towel myself down. I climbed into my shorts and lay down in the sand, letting the sun finish drying me. I was hardly down there before I had fallen asleep. I suppose it was the voices that woke me, but I must have been hearing them for some time before I came properly awake. They were French voices, a woman's and a man's, and they sounded like dream voices. Maybe they intruded on some dream I was having and blended with it, but maybe I heard all that I seemed to be hearing and none of it was dream.

"*La grande Mathilde,*" the woman said.

"Nonsense," the man said. "It can't be."

"But it is. I know her, and Toto knows her. Just see how they are playing. They knew each other at once, as only old friends . . ."

The voices faded out. My eyes popped open and I looked around for the speakers. There were three or four couples with dogs. I was looking for Mathilda. After a moment or two, I spotted her way up the beach racing along shoulder to shoulder with a red setter. They were alone at that end of the beach, Mathilda and Toto—if the setter was Toto. I watched them run, waiting for someone to call in the setter. People who knew Mathilda—I needed to talk to them.

I heard nothing, but the setter stopped short in her running, ramming on her brakes so suddenly that she skidded a few feet and sent fans of loose sand arcing into the air. Reversing her direction, she trotted along. Mathilda pulled up to a less sudden stop and, also turning, ran after the setter. The setter was now moving along at a sedate trot, and Mathilda kept running at it, trying to pull it off into play, but with no success.

Toto was being brought to heel, but I had no way of locating the heel. Nobody had called the dog and nobody was whistling it in. It was, however, obviously responding to a signal, and it was a signal that could do me no good. That dog was being controlled with one of those trick whistles that sounds at a frequency a dog hears but that is beyond the range of a human ear. I was looking from one couple on the beach to another, trying to spot someone who might be blasting away at a silent whistle, but I could see no one like that.

I ran toward the dogs, thinking that I might run alongside them, letting the setter lead me to the people. I had hardly started toward them, however, when the setter ran up onto the walk behind the beach and, crossing it, jumped into a car parked up there by the walk. As soon as the dog had made it, the car took off. I had come nowhere near it. There was a line of benches along the walk there at the top of the beach, and they were between me and the car. It sped along behind that line of benches and turned off out of sight, with never so much as a moment when I could have even tried to catch the license number. Mathilda stayed up there barking at it until it was out of sight and then came waddling back to rejoin me on the sand.

I pulled on my clothes and we started on our round of the cafés. Everything was seeming possible again. Mathilda was in home territory. She'd had her days of running on this beach. She had at least one old friend there. We needed breakfast and the first café along the Boulevard de la Plage seemed as good a place to start as any. It got us nothing but coffee and croissant. The barman and waiters showed no signs of knowing Mathilda, and although they made friendly overtures which she took as her due, she gave no indication that this was a relationship that had any past to it.

"Two American men who had come in one day or more during the lunch hour to make a long-distance telephone call?"

Nothing there. The barman was certain that his phone hadn't been used for any long-distance calls in months.

We pulled out of there. I started for the Porsche, but Mathilda was taking off along the Boulevard on foot and looking back over her shoulder to see if I could be enticed into coming along. She trotted by one café, but at one beyond she turned in. I hurried after her. Inside I found her among friends. The woman who presided over the till had come down from the high perch, the eyrie from which she kept an eagle eye on all café transactions. She was all over Mathilda, and Mathilda was all over her. The barman came hurrying into the act with his offering of an uncooked entrecôte.

Of course they knew Mathilda. It had been some time

since she had last been a daily visitor with Madame and Monsieur; but, of course, she was Madame's dog, and they hadn't been seeing Madame either.

"Monsieur has been around?" I asked, making it as casual as I could.

"Him!" the cashier said.

There was indignation in it and contempt. A couple of hovering waiters exchanged glances and snickered. The cashier fixed them with a stern eye.

"You never know about people," the barman said.

What they had never known about Monsieur and what they thought they had now learned was that he swung both ways. He'd been away, and when he'd come back it had been without Madame. It had been with a man, also an American. The way he behaved with this man, it was to laugh. Right out in public with everyone to see, he was always with his arm around this man. They walked like that. They did everything like that.

"Not that they ever do anything but use the telephone," the cashier said.

"That," said the barman, "is all they ever do in here." His leer indicated the other things he suspected. "They come in during lunch, but not to eat, just to telephone to Dinard."

"Every day?"

I was trying to sound like a connoisseur of strange behavior bent on adding something new to his collection.

"Last week. Twice last week," the cashier said.

"Where are they living?" I asked.

They had no idea.

"I am acting for Madame," I said. "I would like to locate him as quickly as possible."

"Doesn't Madame know?"

"If she knew, I wouldn't have to be trying to find him," I said.

It was true enough in its way. If Barbie hadn't been past knowing anything, I would have had no interest in Gibbs.

Mathilda had disposed of her entrecôte and we pulled out of there. We walked. I was letting Mathilda lead the way. We passed other cafés along the Boulevard. She showed no interest in them. We switched one street back from the beach to the Avenue de Kermario. The cafés back there were fewer, but with them Mathilda gave every evidence of being closer to home territory. She made a stop at each one of them, and in each of them they knew her. They were more modest places than the one on the Boulevard and they brought her more modest offerings. I had to call a halt even on those. She's built too close to the ground for carrying any overweight. It wouldn't take much before she would be scraping.

A few of the cafés back there had also been seeing Gibbs and Elston. They didn't know them by name, but they knew Gibbs in connection with Barbie and Mathilda. In the cafés where they had been seen, it had been for one o'clock phone calls.

Nobody knew where they were living. It had been a couple of days since anyone had last seen them.

Exhausting Kermario, we headed back one more street away from the beach to the Avenue des Druides. There Mathilda took on an air of serious purpose. She had every appearance of a dog who knew where she was going. I followed where she led. It was another café, way out the avenue, just at the edge of town. It was a small place, a one-man operation. Mathilda gave the one man the biggest of her old-buddy greetings. He responded but with reservations.

"Your dog this friendly with everybody?" he asked.

"With people she knows," I said.

"I'm nobody she knows," the man said, "but it's the way I am. Dogs take to me, dogs and women."

"She took to you from way down the road. This was the one place she wanted to come."

"With me dogs are like that," he said. "It must be the way I smell."

I ordered a cognac and knocked it back in a single gulp. That's no way to take cognac, but he could think I didn't know any better. There was one thing I did know. The sooner I could be out of there, the better. This guy was not going to give me anything. He was hostile. It would be no good asking him about two men and phone calls. That would only tip my hand, if it wasn't already tipped.

We pulled out of there, and Mathilda moved purposefully on along the avenue out to where it was dwindling down into a country road. She was obviously following a familiar route, making familiar stops along the way. We were going home and, from the way she was moving and the way the road was going, I was more and more certain that we had made our last wayside stop.

Almost immediately beyond that last café we had run out of sidewalk. Now it was a paved road with a gravel shoulder and a shallow ditch. There was no telling how far we'd have to go. I thought about the Porsche parked back on the Boulevard de la Plage, but it was going to be no good going back to her. No matter how far we'd be going now, there'd be no way we could do it except on foot. We were on the home stretch. Mathilda knew it. She was moving right along without even a moment of hesitation. On foot it was easy. Nothing to it but behaving as though I was the one who had been to obedience school. I had only to come to heel and follow along dutifully, taking my lead from Mathilda.

Walking that road, we had to keep an eye out for cars, but we were encountering almost none of those. I looked at my watch. Of course it was that time of day when this whole great country would be at lunch. My watch verified it. Noon had just been and gone.

There were houses along the road, but Mathilda was showing no interest in them. As we went along, the houses were thinning out. After a little more than a kilometer we were in open country.

Mathilda raced off ahead of me. To look at her, seeing her short legs and sinuous waddle, you'd never think she was built for speed. Nevertheless, when she had a mind to, she could move. I'm not setting her up for outrunning anyone's greyhound, but I had to break into a gallop even to keep her in sight.

She came to a small side road and she whipped around into it. Although, once she was off the road, I couldn't see her, I could still keep track of where she was, because now I could hear her. Mathilda was giving tongue.

She was barking. I had come to know the various ways she sounded. I recognized this for happy barking. It reminded me of the morning and the romp she'd had with the setter on Carnac Plage. I was guessing that she had now come upon another four-footed old buddy. I was listening for an answering bark. With the red setter, after all, it had been a dialogue.

I heard no answering bark, but Mathilda was not going unanswered. What I heard was a shot, and then another, and then a third. I was listening for some sudden yelp of pain or a sharp cutoff of the barking. Gibbs was down that side road waiting for us. I'd been right about that last café.

Gibbs had been phoned a warning. I would reach this turnoff Mathilda had taken, and he would be down in there with his gun trained on that road entrance. The first instant I showed, he would gun me down.

He had a perfect setup there and he was spoiling it for himself, unless you want to think Mathilda was spoiling it for him. The dog had been taking me to him. Okay. He knocks off the dog and I'm nowhere, except that he's too late for that. There can't be so many houses up this little road. I can still check them out to zero in on one of them. A kidnaper doesn't choose a place where he has many neighbors.

I had come too close. Even without Mathilda I could go the rest of the way. That is, I could if I stayed alive. Because of Mathilda I was going to have a good chance of it. Her barking had him spotted for me. His shooting was telling me what I was up against.

I had to move and move fast. The picture was clear enough. Mathilda had found him. Mathilda was overjoyed. For her it was a reunion. I could imagine her grinning all over as she jumped for him. He was an old friend, and Mathilda could hardly be expected to understand that he was no longer a friend. Dogs don't change sides. How can you ask a dog to know that, of the many ways men differ from dogs, this is one?

She was jumping at him and he was getting those shots off, one after another, shooting at her. Thus far he had been missing, but he couldn't be expected to go on missing forever, or even for long. I was going to have to catch up with him before he got off the shot that wouldn't miss. It was for Mathilda's sake and for my own.

Why it would be for Mathilda's sake was obvious. For my own, there had come to me a sudden understanding of all that gunfire. He'd had me ambushed. He'd been in there waiting for me to come into his sights, but Mathilda was spoiling that. She was in there telling me he was there and just where I was to look for him. If he could still succeed in getting off the shot that would silence the pup, he could make a quick change of position and re-establish his ambush. It could be almost as good as it had been. I would know he was in there waiting and ready, but I wouldn't have Mathilda to tell me just where.

I jumped the roadside ditch. The road along there was running through lightly wooded country. I dove into the woods and ran toward the barking and the sound of the shots. I would have liked it a lot if I could have done the last-of-the-Mohicans bit and gone sliding through those woods invisibly and silently, betraying myself by not so much as the snapping of a twig or the rustling of a leaf. I had no time for that. I just had to go crashing through, making the best possible time.

Against all expectations, the noise of my progress didn't matter. I had noise cover. You'd have to know those great barks Mathilda hauls up all the way from the toes of her hind paws. Neither the snapping of twigs nor the breaking of branches packs nearly enough decibels to compete.

I came in behind him. He was in the woods just off that little side road. He was using a tree trunk for cover and some shrubbery for concealment, but this was cover and concealment to serve him against an adversary coming at him by road. For his rear he had no protection.

I drew my confiscated revolver. I took careful aim. I would have liked to do something fancy like shooting the gun out of his hand, but I was settling for something surer, even if it was less spectacular. I got him in the shoulder. The slug spun him around and knocked him off his feet.

Mathilda ran in. Enthusiastically she licked his face. He wasn't appreciating it, but there wasn't much he could do about it. The gun had fallen from his hand.

I started toward them. Since she couldn't lick and bark at the same time, silence had fallen on the patch of woods. Hearing me, he looked up and spotted me as I was coming in on him. Holding Mathilda off with his left hand—his right wasn't good for much with my slug in that shoulder—he snapped an order at her. I'd seen Barbie put the pup through her obedience-school paces, but this was a new command, a trick they had never shown me.

"Take him, Matt," he said.

The dog wheeled toward me with her teeth bared. An unthinking reflex brought my gun up, but that was as far as it went. Thought jumped in and stopped my trigger finger. Some similar thought must have jumped at Mathilda. She kept coming, but the snarl converted into one of the most rollicking of her grins, and her charge wasn't one of those arrow-straight lunges I had seen those times when she had gone into action. It was another of those joyous wiggles in which her wagging tail takes command.

Gibbs cursed her, and the poor bewildered pup ran back and forth between us, trying to ladle out love in equal portions. Gibbs wanted none of it. When she ran at him, he kicked out at her. It didn't bother her any. It might have been a new kind of game. I grabbed him and jerked him to his feet.

"Take it easy," he said. "You win."

"I want Elston."

"Tonight."

"Right now."

"Right now's no good to anybody. Tonight I collect. Tonight I was going to hand him over to his people. Okay. You win. Tonight I hand him over to you and we split on the ransom."

"You'll need a doctor to take the slug out of your shoulder," I said. "The flics will get you one."

He shook his head.

"I know a doctor. He'll take it out. He asks no questions and he makes no reports."

"I couldn't care less about Elston," I said.

"Then, what's this for? What do you want?"

"I want you. This is for her. You shouldn't have killed her."

"I had to."

"Why? She wasn't letting you down. She was all out protecting you."

"That wasn't going to last. She knew too much about me. For a dame in another guy's bed, she knew too much."

I didn't want to listen to any more of that.

"Where have you got him?" I asked.

"You can go screw."

That was just for his pride or something. I didn't need him. Mathilda had brought me too close.

"Your play's been stupid all the way," I told him. "You've been letting Elston see you. You let yourself be seen with him in a whole flock of cafés. His secretary knew who you were from your first call. He knows your voice. Even if you collected the ransom, how far were you going to get with it?"

"With a million bucks a man can do a lot of getting lost," he said.

There wasn't only the one house up that back road, but there was only one that wasn't boarded up and empty. He had Elston locked in the cellar, but Elston was in good shape and didn't seem to mind. Elston had cards. When we came in on him, he was playing solitaire.

He didn't mind being rescued, but he wasn't wildly enthusiastic about it either.

"He'd be collecting the ransom and turning me loose tonight," he said. "It would have been last night if not for those Commie farmers and their crazy strike. They blocked all the roads with cabbages. How's that for crazy?"

"So now he's turning you loose without collecting," I said.

Elston shrugged.

"No difference," he said. "We've been playing gin all the time and I've been winning. I've won almost all of it back from him even before it's been paid. I hold his IOUs."

Could you believe that? I couldn't.

"And you expected he'd pay you?" I asked.

"He's a gambler," Elston said. "He's a pro. They don't welch."

"He's a killer," I said. "Maybe he wasn't going to welch on that."

Gibbs was saying nothing.

Elston, that dope, was speaking for him.

"He never once mistreated me," he said.

"You can tell that to the judge when he comes to trial," I said. "It should win him a hunk of clemency, like they'll maybe put him away for only one lifetime or, at worst, two lifetimes served concurrently."

Elston shook his head.

"We're letting him go," he said. He turned to Gibbs. "You take off," he said. "We'll stay here, Erridge and me, and we won't surface until you're well away. How much time do you need?"

"Twenty-four hours," Gibbs said. "Like till this time tomorrow."

"Okay," Elston said. "This time tomorrow. Go on, take off." He turned to me. "I hope you play gin," he said.

"I won't need to."

That one went past Elston, but Gibbs got it. He wasn't

moving, not while I had the gun on him, but he did try it on.

"How about it?" he asked.

"Don't try it," I said. "I'll shoot you in the legs and I'll enjoy doing it."

"It was him I snatched. It's no skin off *your* ass."

"Barbie," I said.

"That was no skin off you either. She'd already run out on you."

"Who's Barbie?" Elston asked.

"She was my girl," I said.

It didn't quite get over, because Gibbs was talking at the same time and he was saying much the same thing.

"And he murdered her," I added.

That did get over.

"You did that?" Elston asked Gibbs.

Gibbs shrugged.

"A crime of passion," he said. "Hell, man, this is France."

Elston turned away from him.

"Anywhere," he said, "you shouldn't have done that."

There was a phone in the house. I had known there would be. It wasn't only the warning he'd had from the guy in the café. It was also that Barbie had called him that morning from Vernon. I called the gendarmes. They came and took him off my hands.

Mathilda wailed a bit when they took him away and she couldn't follow to the lockup; but, once he was out of sight, she seemed to get over it. She's happy with me. She doesn't miss him. I don't think she even misses Barbie.

That puts her one up on me. I do.